THE ZODIAN WARRIOR

CHAOS CURSE BOOK I

CHAOS CURSE BOOK 1

Copyright © 2023 by Kasey LeAlma

Contact info: kasey@kaseylealma.com

www.kaseylealma.com

www.instagram.com/kaseylealma

Published by: Moon Witch Books, LLC

Cover Design by: GetCovers.com

Formatting by: Green Spark Publishing

Editor: Jeanine Harrell, Indie Edits with Jeanine

ISBN: 978-1-961587-00-7 (E-book)

ISBN: 978-1-961587-01-4 (Paperback)

First Edition: September 2023

KASEY LEALMA

CHAOS CURSE BOOK I

I want to thank Aunt Wanda for giving the advice to "write what you know."

Unfortunately for her, that was witches, vampires, and demons.

Heath Ellington climbed the stained stairs. He peered down at the level below through the gap between the wall and the landing. *How did this place continue to stand?* He'll need to have another talk with Makani about moving out of this creature-infested neighborhood. He continued down the hall, kids scattering at the sight of him. Even in plain clothes, they sensed his hatred.

He entered the one-bedroom apartment where Makani, his girlfriend, waited with their daughter. He surveyed the room. The hair raised on his arms. The mess. Toys that usually littered the floor were now gone. Everything in its place.

She approached from the bedroom, Ember hanging on her hip. He turned toward her. Every day he stood in awe of her beauty, creamy complexion, red-stained lips, with sunflower hair — the day Makani agreed to have coffee with him was his luckiest. That first year had been amazing. There was only one obstacle to their perfection, but it was only a matter of time before he could cure her of her darkness.

"I'm leaving."

He focused on her lips. *Full, ripe lips.*

"Heath, I'm leaving."

"What?" He said, "You can't leave."

She tensed, clutching Ember tighter in her arms. Bags on her shoulder. She was really leaving. *She couldn't.*

"You can't leave me. We will be perfect for each other."

"We could never be perfect for each other. I've found my Cara Anu, and you're not him."

"What?" He asked. "That makes no sense. What about us? All of this time? Our child? You can't take my daughter," he bit out, standing in front of her, blocking the door.

Her dewy eyes softened. "What if she's not your daughter?"

Pain spasmed around his heart. The truth he couldn't deny stared up at him. Ember's violet eyes and darker complexion proved she was not at all like him. *He'd known.* He wanted to be wrong.

"Liar," he screamed.

"I'm sorry," she said softly. "I know you don't understand. He died. I know now that I shouldn't have. I was lost." She stepped forward. "I can't stay here, Heath. Please let us go."

He thrust his arms wide. "You're not leaving."

He watched the darkness come over her. Her once dewy eyes sharpened. Ember wailed at the loud tones.

"You can't stop me," she hissed out as she bounced Ember on her hip.

The air around Heath shifted. He tensed at her show of strength. The wind gusted in the apartment, swirling around them. She stood tall as the air lifted them off the floor. Reversing their places.

She reached for the doorknob and whispered, "Good-bye, Heath."

The air rushed out of the room behind her. Leaving nothing but stillness and the stale stench of this rotting place.

Heath sank into the chair, hair clawing at his eyes as the tears descended. *How could she leave me? We could have been good together.* He would have raised that girl, *his* daughter, better than anyone. They would have been a perfect family.

He reached for his phone and dialed the one number that could possibly bring her back.

"Mom, we won't be needing the cure. She left me . . ."

". . . Heath." Her voice came through the darkness.

He looked up to see his mother standing in the doorway. In her arms was Ember.

"Ember!" He rushed over to take the child from her. He checked her over. "Where's Makani?"

His mother spoke tight-lipped, "She didn't make it."

"What happened?" His voice croaked.

"Couldn't be helped," she quipped. "One less creature running amok."

Makani was gone. *Had I caused her death?* He cuddled the little girl in his arms. She was his daughter now.

"I'll take good care of you, Ember," he whispered.

"Emma," his mother said, handing over a vial.

Heath took the cure. The dark liquid swirled, and he knew his mother was right. "Emma."

His mother nodded and turned to leave. "Let's get out of this hellhole."

When the door opened, the screams reached his ears. He stepped out into the hallway.

"What's going on?" he asked, pulling Emma closer to him.

His mother smiled for the first time. "We're cleaning house."

One

EMBER

Suffocation hit me as I glanced over to the passenger seat. The birthday present ensconced there. Waiting to be opened. Ready to be consumed. I unraveled the bow from the small box. The dark liquid gleamed under the light. I shuddered at the implication and retied the bow.

I slid out of the car to wait for Grace under the single light post beside the faded red barn next to her house. I looked over at the two-story farmhouse silhouetted by the moon, with an attached garage sitting on forty acres of land. I remembered the nights spent there laughing into the wee hours — *our small window of freedom*. The last time I saw her was during the summer when we took an afternoon to sunbathe in her backyard. The prior four years had been a strain on our friendship.

When I called earlier to ask for a favor, I didn't know if she would agree. The most we talked on the phone since was probably five minutes. Text messages were almost as scarce. We'd been friends for thirteen years, and I never thought that would waver. When she answered, I stuttered before asking if she would meet me at three in the morning.

"Em."

I turned to her. "Hey."

The lump grew in my throat, and I pulled her into my arms. Lightness sang in my heart as her warmth touched me. I didn't know how much I needed her until now.

Grace was fun incarnate with her bleach-blonde curls and her signature bright red lipstick. She hadn't changed her bouncy style in all the years I'd known her despite her parents' efforts to tame her. If I was having the worst day, her bubbly personality would pull me out. *Every damn time.*

"It's late," she complained as her arms tightened around me. "I'm so glad you're back."

I pulled away, but the bracelet around my right wrist caught in her hair. "Hold on, don't move."

We giggled as Grace squirmed under the first few attempts to untangle the cuff.

"I can't believe you still wear that."

"Dammit, hold still," I muttered. Once I freed Grace's hair, I stepped away and placed my hand in the back pocket of my jeans. "I've had it for years. I don't even notice it anymore."

"Unless it gets caught in people's hair," Grace said, tilting her head. "Does it ever get stuck in yours?"

I laughed. "Of course." My black hair was straight and thin, but the cuff's snaps could get stuck in any type.

Grace yawned. "Why'd we meet so late?"

"When I called twenty minutes ago, you were still up. What were you doing? Reading?" It was amazing how five minutes of conversation could make the last four years fade away.

"That was twenty minutes ago."

I rolled my eyes.

"What's so important?" she asked.

I walked around the car and stopped at the open passenger side window. "I need a favor with no questions."

She followed. "Will you tell me someday?"

I didn't know if I ever wanted to tell her about this side of me. Especially if I chose it one day. But I couldn't bring it home. *Not yet.* I plucked the box out of the front seat and held it out to her.

"What's this?" she asked, rubbing the white ribbon between her fingers and reading the note Dad had placed there.

I'd read it thousands of times before. *Happy Birthday. Love, Dad.*

"It's a box I need you to hold for a while." Her hand clasped around it. "*Without* opening it."

"You're no fun," she teased but nodded. "I'll put it in my closet and forget about it."

"Thanks, Grace. This means a lot."

She pursed her lips. "You seem more relaxed, way different from high school." She smiled a little.

I didn't know how to respond, but then she kept going.

"When will you have time to catch up? I have so much to tell you, and I know you will *not* believe me." Grace's smile spread, and she started pulsing from one foot to the next.

A shiver ran down my spine, and my chest tightened. "What is it?" I stepped forward as the wind whipped past us.

She shook her head. "Not now. I'm too tired, and you need to go home to your dad." She smiled as she turned toward the house, calling over her shoulder, "When he lets you out again, call me." She held the box up as a salute before disappearing into the house.

I followed her example, holding my hand in farewell, even though her back was to me, and thinking over what she said. There was a good chance it would be a while before I left home again. I climbed into my car and headed down the lane.

What have I done?

Had I made the right choice two years ago? I gripped the steering wheel until my knuckles turned white. The truth mattered right now. I needed to know my mother's past. Her people. And Dad had those answers.

Grace would keep my secrets as she had in high school. The tension in my shoulders eased as I drove the rest of the way home.

I staggered up the stairs of Dad's ranch-style one-and-a-half-story house with my backpack, rolling suitcase, archery gear, and duffle bag. I reached for the keys in my pocket. The bags shifted. *One load.* I laughed as I set the bags on the top step. Before I could unlock the door, it opened.

"A minute too late," I uttered.

My chest tightened as Dad stood in the doorway. Our relationship was complicated, but I had missed him. He appeared older than his forty-one years. His hair was thinner on top since the last time I saw him with a dusting of gray.

I'd come home one day on Christmas three years ago and was barely able to do anything before he ushered me back to Berkeley to spend the rest of vacation with Vanessa, my college roommate.

He laughed as he stepped outside. His hand came down on my shoulder. "Welcome home, Emma."

I winced at the sound of that name. He didn't seem to notice or remember the number of times I'd asked him to stop using the name he'd picked instead of my birth name. It was innocently revealed that my name wasn't Emma during one of those rare visits from Gran, Mom's mother. She used to come to read me bedtime stories, but that was before we moved to Happy Valley.

"Let's get you inside." He grabbed the archery bag and the rolling suitcase while I gathered the rest.

We carried the luggage through the one-and-a-half-story house and crossed the landing to my old room. Dad dropped the bags as I looked around. The bed sat in the corner with the dresser mirror combo directly in front of it. Posters of boy bands lined the walls as the faded glow-in-the-dark stars mocked my constellation frenzy phase. Four years had changed nothing and everything. My shoulders sagged. *I'm home.*

He smiled. "You can unpack tomorrow." He grasped my right hand, covering the bracelet underneath, and pulled me closer. "I'm glad you're finally home. Ready for your future. Don't worry about anything."

My future. What did that mean? He called good night as he left the room. *Did he know?* I shook my head as I climbed into my full-size bed. The faded stars twinkled down at me. *Had coming home been a mistake?*

The four o'clock hour pressed against me, but sleep didn't come easily. What had Dad meant? Ugh, I needed to tell him. Based on the look in his eye when he said "future," my choice would crush him. I couldn't tell him yet. I needed to see how he responded to the questions.

It wasn't like I meant to get my magic back, but I couldn't deny the wholeness I felt after my birthday two years ago. It had been unexpected. Even after all the lectures I'd received growing up, I didn't want to prove Dad wrong. But I needed to understand who I was. If that meant lying to him right now, then I would. Hopefully the old saying of asking forgiveness instead of permission held true.

I reached up, turned the light off, and snuggled on top of the bed. I raised my hand toward the glowing green stars but grasped nothing. The aether was quiet as well. I brought my hand down and snapped my fingers. A flame sparked but died out. *Must be because I'm home.* I took a deep breath in and out. The aether told me no one was around, but the instinct to hide who I was consumed me.

I'd come home to get answers, but I also needed to hide that I hadn't taken the elixir from Dad. My plan was to fall back into the role I played before leaving for college in the hopes of Dad answering my questions. Once I knew more about who I was, I would tell him. *I would.* I just needed time. Another breath in and out before snapping my fingers again. This time my flame appeared. I smiled as I made shapes in the darkness. One calm breath later, I released the fire back to the universe.

Sleep followed soon after.

Two

EMBER

The sweat-drenched sheets clung to me. Before I remembered that I was *home*, bright light burst through the sheer curtains. I sighed and rolled onto my side, covering my eyes, but the sounds of birds chirping outside the window drove me to sit up.

Dad's house was in a well-established neighborhood in Happy Valley. He had worked as an assistant to a realtor and single-handedly raised me while earning his license. I knew being a single Dad had been hard for him. Especially with a temperamental child like me.

I grabbed my phone from the nightstand to find the time. *Lunchtime.* I climbed out of bed, tripped over one of the bags, and landed with a thud on my knees. Groaning, I opened it and started to unpack.

Mr. Rabbit stared at me as I zipped around the room, putting clothes away despite the fact I wouldn't be here that long. I placed the last piece of clothing in the dresser drawer and picked him up. He was discolored from age and the amount of love one lonely stuffed animal could get throughout the years.

On the bottom of one foot was a tiny charred spot. Mr. Rabbit had to sit beside the open window for weeks in order to cure the smoke smell. Dad's lips pursed as he'd scrubbed the only animal that ever comforted me. It had been the first disappointment. He'd thrown it into the washing machine, which destroyed the other leg, and I despaired over the bunny's death until Grace's mom sewed the leg back onto its body.

"It's been through a lot, maybe you should throw it out now. I came to see if you wanted to head out to the range? Meet you in ten."

I glanced at the open doorway where Dad's back faced me as he walked away before gaining my acceptance. *Ugh.* I pulled out a change of clothes, and I hid Mr. Rabbit in the drawer.

Dad stood beside the SUV tapping his foot as I handed him my archery equipment to load into the back.

"Here you go, Sport," he said, pushing the button on the key to unlock the doors as he walked past.

Once the seatbelt clicked, Dad put the car in gear and pulled out of the driveway. On our way to the north side of the city, we cruised through downtown. This historical area housed a few upscale restaurants, the bank I worked at in high school, and the old courthouse. The gun range came into view a mile outside city limits. We had a paid membership for as long as I could remember.

Neither one of us used guns, but the open space gave us an opportunity to practice archery. Few used the range as actively as we did. I came twice a day before I left for college, and Dad came once a day, at least in my youth. Most days he taught me archery, but other days he taught me self-defense.

I headed to my favorite spot, thankful no one else was there. I strapped on the quiver and sat the bow case down in the last booth, where I still had a full view of the parking lot. It had been three weeks since I'd picked up this bow. Hopefully Dad wouldn't notice.

"What's your favorite color, Emma?" Dad asked while I caught up on schoolwork. The next month, he gifted me a compound bow made for my build and strength with a purple carbon fiber limb. I instantly loved it, despite the extra early mornings that came with it.

I stood angled toward the target with my knees shoulder width apart before taking a deep breath. *One, two, three.* The arrow landed dead center. *Thank God.*

"Perfect as always," Dad chimed beside me.

He prepared his first arrow, and I watched it soar through the air.

I smiled. "You're a little off, Dad." I aimed for my next target, which was one-hundred twenty feet away.

"Don't miss," he whispered the moment my arrow released.

I turned to smile at him when the arrow hit dead center again.

"Show off. You've had more practice."

"You don't come out here?" I asked, glancing around the perimeter. Back behind us were woods that led into the city. When the wind blew through the tall grass that bordered the other three sides, it whistled magically.

He waited until his arrow landed three inches to the side, like last time, before he turned to me. "No, I say this is good for not coming out here in four years."

Four years? He stopped coming when I left town. I searched his face, but no answers revealed themselves. "Why? you loved archery."

I couldn't see his expression when he answered. "The archery was for you. For you to learn control and seeing you today, I know the lessons helped."

Me? Yes, because I couldn't control my anger. Archery lessons had begun with meditation, balanced breathing, and calmness to control the anger within that could destroy me. But wasn't that the purpose of the gift? I held a deep breath as I jerked the arrows from my quiver in rapid succession. Willing the anger to hit the mark. All three dead center.

"You're amazing. I never imagined that you would take to this so well." He paused. "Your mother had perfect aim too." His voice sounded enthralled as his eyes turned to the sky.

He offered the opening, and I took it. I spent the drive home yesterday going over different ways to approach this topic, but none seemed right. "I want to know more about her. I don't know anything about her past or how old she was when she died. What was her favorite color? Did she like archery as much as I do?"

I patiently waited for his answer, prayed for it. This

felt right, this felt like a beginning. He would tell me. He had to. *Twenty-two years.* It was time I knew my mother.

"That's not part of your future, Emma." His voice, like a razor blade, sliced through me.

That name, *Emma*, though it sounded right, made my skin crawl. It wasn't me, not anymore. Not since I'd left for college. Why had I let this continue? Why hadn't I stood up to him years ago?

The fire rose inside me. "My name is Ember." I stepped back from him. "I need to know her." My voice grew louder, pulse pounding. Losing control now would be the worst mistake I could make. I turned toward the parking lot, my vision blurred and chest constricted. *Breathe. Just breathe. Everything will be fine.*

A gentle hand on my shoulder told me he'd moved closer. "Why does it matter? I've called you Emma your entire life."

I choked out the sob, "It's the only piece of her I have."

"Shh." He pulled me into him, and we swayed back and forth. "I can call you Ember if I must. To honor Makani."

"Thank you," I whispered into his shirt, shoulders relaxing as relief flooded me.

Would he open up to me? I sighed, clinging to the hope as if I could hold onto this moment.

The drive back to town seemed to take forever. I wanted to shower and go back to bed. The last time I had spent four hours at the range was six weeks ago when I was preparing for a school competition my scholarship required. While I enjoyed archery, on so little sleep, it drove home the fact that it was a workout.

"Sore, old man?" I asked after Dad rubbed his shoulder.

He shook his head.

"You should probably admit that I won today." I smiled as he looked at me.

"I have a surprise."

"Okay?"

Berkeley had been the last surprise he'd sprung on me. Before that, there had been new equipment, instructors, and meditation lessons when I turned six. None of that had helped. Not until he found the precious elixir. I stared down at the bracelet that had been my mother's. It hid the discolored birthmark that looked more like a tattoo. It had been years since I truly looked at the mark. I would never forget the intricacies of the five triangles connected in a circle imprinted on my flesh.

"I went to the bank today before coming home," Dad said.

I groaned and slipped my phone under my leg, silencing a phone call from Grace. "They need someone to fill a spot. The manager said you could come back to work."

"But," I started, trying to reason that working as a teller wasn't what I wanted.

"You don't have any plans, and while we don't need the money, it would be good for you to get out of the house."

"I was planning to get out of the house. I haven't seen Grace in four years, or Hannah."

"You can't spend all your time with those girls. Don't they both have jobs and lives? You need your own life. You need to look toward a better future."

I shifted in the seat, leaning against the door, propping my head against the coldness of the glass window. It was true Grace had a job and wouldn't be able to spend all day with me, not like I had wanted to anyway. But once the history of my family was settled, I could go work for Vanessa's cousin, Evie, back in Berkeley. It was a standing offer I could take any time in the future.

I turned to plead with him. Meeting his eyes, I knew I had already lost. I sunk lower into the seat, staring out the window, watching houses pass.

"What time are we going for a run in the morning?"

I groaned as I lifted to look at his face. He smiled at me. *Seriously. Damn.* I tried to smile as I worked through reasons why running at the crack of dawn was not in my best interests. But if I stayed on his good side, I could get answers faster. I knew from childhood that staying in line was much easier on me. Eventually, it helped me sneak out after he went to bed at night.

"Could we do five-thirty instead of four-thirty?"

He laughed. "Of course, but we better stop by the bank before it closes to talk to the manager." The click of the turn signal sounded in the car as he maneuvered the

SUV around the courthouse of downtown Happy Valley where the bank sat on the west side.

In the morning hours before the light slipped into the sky, we headed out for our jog through the surrounding neighborhoods. While I wasn't out of shape, sprinting next to someone who was addicted to running made for an extremely exhausting pace.

"Slow down," I yelled ahead of me.

Dad sprinted farther ahead, acting like he couldn't hear me. I pushed my limbs harder, ignoring the burn. *I'm not letting him beat me.* A familiar blue house came into my vision, and I stopped in the middle of the road, staring. Luke's house. Thoughts of winning fled my mind.

The picture-perfect two-story home stood silent, dark among the rising sun behind it. The paint on the white shutters and yellow door were cracked and faded. No light shone through the house, not even in the kitchen where Luke's mom would start her day. Something was wrong with this picture. What had happened?

Dad ran back down the street and stopped beside my frozen frame.

"What happened here?"

"Nothing," he said quietly. "Nothing you need to worry about."

I turned toward him, hearing the secret in his voice. "No, it's something." My voice came out harsh, but I needed to know what had happened.

"A car accident," he blurted. "Helen and Thomas Bowen died."

The stiffness in the air held me hostage as I tried to breathe through those words. Luke's parents were dead.

"And Luke?" my voice wavered.

I clamped a hand over my mouth. I looked around the empty street before my eyes caught Dad's stare.

"You still have feelings for him?" he asked, his eyes narrowed at me.

Of course, I have feelings for him. We dated for three of the four years of high school.

"He's a friend." I said after a short pause, "Is he okay?"

Dad sighed. "I don't know. He vanished."

"Vanished?" How was that possible?

He sighed again and turned to look down the road before he responded. "No one has truly seen Luke since it happened. I don't know who's running his father's real estate developer company either."

"When?" How had I not heard about this? *Why didn't Grace tell me?*

"His birthday, two and a half years ago."

The same time my fire emerged. Was this the news Grace had wanted to tell me the other night? "January third," I muttered.

Dad turned to me but didn't comment. How awful to lose both your parents on a day meant for celebration. Minutes passed as I stared at the unkempt, somber house.

Finally, Dad tugged me down the street.

Three

EMBER

I stood in the breakroom of Happy Valley's First Bank, staring down at the plastic badge which held the same picture I'd taken in high school. And honestly it seemed like I was back in that time. I had allowed Dad to set up our old strenuous workout and meditation routine, and with Dad's schedule, the last month went by faster than I imagined. It left no time for anything else. I huffed and slid the badge onto my blouse.

A beep sounded, and I spun to see Hannah swiping her own card. "Hannah?"

She pulled me into a tight hug. "About time you came home, Em."

"I thought you'd never come back here after college," I said, reciting parts of the speech she spewed at the cheerleaders during our last pep rally.

She laughed. "Shit happened a little differently than I expected."

"I'm sorry I didn't keep in touch." We exchanged a

few likes and comments on social media, but I had basically cut all ties to Happy Valley when I drove out of town that hot June day. Especially after Grace stopped responding to messages.

She shrugged. "It happens, girl." She pulled off her nametag. "Wait, are you starting back here?"

"I've been back for a month. Dad pulled some strings."

Hannah fist-pumped the air. "Awesome! I've been on vacation, and then Doug's grandma got sick and passed away. I haven't worked that much this past month. I didn't even see your name on the schedule."

I pointed to the schedule. "It's because my full name is on here and not just Em. Sorry about Doug's grandma."

She nodded as she peered at the paper on the wall. "Oh my gosh. I always thought your name was Emma, but Em's short for Ember. That's way cool."

I laughed, knowing she probably heard Dad say Emma on occasion and Emma had been printed on school forms, but I'd always asked the teachers to call me Em.

"What happened to Portland?"

Hannah was extremely fun when she'd been around, but she'd spent most of high school with her boyfriend, Doug.

Hannah snapped her fingers together. "Hated every minute of it. We should get together and have a girl's night. Have you seen Grace yet?"

That made sense, I'd hardly ever seen her without

Doug. "Not yet. We have a date tonight at Casa del Pecado. Would you be able to make it?"

"Shoot. Doug's family is getting together to go through some of his gram's things. But we should still do something soon. I haven't seen Grace since her aunt and uncle passed away in that horrible car accident."

I tensed. Luke and Grace were cousins. After finding out, I'd texted them both, but only Grace had responded. She had stated grief had torn him apart, which was no shock. Luke and his parents had been a close-knit family.

Hannah continued, "I think the last time we hung out was her twenty-first birthday, and then after that, she got dodgy. I thought she had a secret f-boi."

I laughed, and we reminisced about the many times Grace said she'd find a guy with money to support her many shopping trips. It usually coincided with when her mom would take her cards in an effort to teach her good money habits. We chatted until the manager broke us up and I headed to start my shift.

I couldn't wait to see Grace tonight after work. We planned to drink margaritas and chill together. Time to catch up was well overdue, considering how busy Dad made sure I was. I couldn't help it though; I needed answers from him. I'd have to play by his rules, even if five o'clock running sucked ass. Grace always understood. She'd dealt with my dad almost as long as I had.

On my first day at school in Happy Valley, I had been swinging by myself as I watched the other kids play until a bossy girl had pushed me off. After Grace scared the other little girl away, she told me we would be the best of friends. And we had been nearly inseparable until Berkeley.

I also had my suspicions that Dad didn't want me to hang out with her. Though I couldn't figure out why.

"Excuse me," a voice jolted me out of my thoughts.

I glanced at the white-haired lady. "How can I help you?" I heard the irritation in my voice, and I widened my smile in the hopes the manager didn't catch it.

"I need to deposit this check."

I grabbed a new deposit slip from the side stash, but before I could set it down, the lady plopped her checkbook on the counter. *Guess I'll fill out the slip for her.* I wrote her name and number on the slip.

"Do you have the check?" I asked.

She dug around in her purse, then emptied the contents on the counter instead. A quarter rolled past me, but I snatched it up and placed it back within her reach. She sifted through the new and used tissues, peppermint candies, and receipts to find the check.

I dragged my hand, waiting for the check. *Gross.* I wiped my hands on my jeans before writing the amount down. "Do you need any cash withdrawn today?"

She grumbled and wagged her hand back and forth, so I typed in the transaction. I sighed a breath of relief when the old lady walked out.

While the bank job had not been my choice, it *wasn't that* bad. Four hours each day of the week left me plenty of time to practice. And now, with Hannah, the days would be better.

Some days I felt like I was still that eighteen-year-old

girl that knew nothing of the world. I'd completely dropped back into the good-daughter role. Each day my questions and retorts were bubbling to the surface, ready to explode. I retreated to the range whenever it got tough. There I would concentrate on controlling my powers.

Practice started with meditation—*at this rate*, I should be a *fucking* certified coach. I was lucky Lyra agreed to meet with me regularly on the phone. Though it seemed way easier in person. She was something in between a mentor and friend, yelling her instructions through the phone and expecting me to understand how to control the fire within me. This morning I stopped to pick up candles for training since it wasn't going well. I'd burned through the last batch at lightning speed.

In the two years I'd known her, she almost topped Dad for demanding schedules. But I knew I needed this.

I had talked my friends into going out a day earlier to celebrate my twenty-first birthday. At the stroke of midnight, like in Cinderella, my fire emerged. It wasn't until days later when I had misunderstood Dad's gift, but it had been too late. While having fire appear abruptly, scorching pillows and clothes, my heart had been full. The underlying anger and energy vibrating below my skin disappeared.

I needed to reconcile the fear that had been preached over the years with the truth.

I needed to find another like me.

My Gran's stories surfaced. Zodians lived in tribes, and she had spoken about their community near Berkeley.

A quick search of landmarks from the stories brought me to the outer city with cookie-cutter houses.

A gated community. I hesitated in front of the guard-house. This was it. They could have answers. Before I could take a step closer to the entrance, a guard stepped outside his post.

"Are you lost?" he asked, hands on the side of his enlarged stomach.

I stilled at the hostility in his voice.

"Are you lost?" he repeated, taking a step toward me.

The liquor on his breath forced me back a step. "I'm looking for the–" I searched for the perfect word. "Tribal leader."

"What nonsense," the guard said, turning to walk away.

"Please, sir, I need to talk to someone. A Zodian." Taking several steps closer, I sputtered the last word.

He stopped; his eyes leveled on mine. "Nonsense, this is a private community, and they don't need your crazy."

"I'm not crazy," I shouted, thrusting my arms out as the heat rose around me. "I need some help." My anxiety-filled mind rummaged for a solution.

With his arms back on his hips, he pushed me back with his stomach. "If you don't leave, I will call the police."

His threat worked. I couldn't afford to get arrested. Not now. I stepped back and turned, heading the way I came.

Halfway down the sidewalk, I had begun to calm myself. The tickle at the back of my neck told me I was being watched. Every time I turned to survey the area, it was deserted. The bus was in the distance. If I jogged the rest of the way, I could catch it.

A person stepped out in front of me.

I skidded to a stop and placed a hand over my racing heart. The person blocking my way stood tall with black hair and deep violet eyes. I cocked my head at the newcomer. I'd never met another person with violet eyes. She waited for my inspection to be over. Heat crept up my cheeks.

"I'm sorry. You startled me," I said, trying to get a handle on this. Whatever this was.

"I heard you wanted to talk to the Shaman," she said as she walked around me. "He's old and boring."

I turned, losing sight of her before she stood in front of me again.

"I'm not boring."

No, she didn't look boring. She wore tight, high-waisted leather pants the color of blood, with a pristine white silk blouse that had puffy sleeves and a black choker around her neck.

"I'm sorry." I tried to get my words out. "I'm late for the bus." The bus was idle at the intersection ahead.

"Zodians aren't cowards," she whispered, but I heard her perfectly.

I turned to face her; the bus forgotten. "Who are you?"

She smiled. "I'm Lyra."

"Girl." A sharp tone startled me.

She never was boring. I smiled as the memory faded, bringing me back to the white, clinical walls of the bank.

The old man stood tensed with his hand palmed down on the counter.

"Yes, sir."

"I need to make a deposit in my savings, not my checking."

Of course. I tore up the paper slip I originally grabbed and set it aside to trash it later. I yanked the new deposit slip, writing his information.

"How much do you want in savings?" I asked, not trying to hide the irritation in my voice.

"Do you have the account?" he asked, eyeing me from across the bars that separated the teller line from the lobby.

"This is your number, correct?" I slid the savings slip toward him. He looked and nodded as I asked again, "How much do you want in savings?"

"Um, let me see." He looked at the check. "Fifty."

"Of course. No problem."

I wrote the fifty, did the math for the rest, and handed him the slip. He signed before I processed the transaction. By the time I finished the clock showed after four o'clock in the afternoon. I sighed. Time for friends. I was so ready for a laughter-filled night. Even if Hannah wouldn't be able to join us tonight, Grace and I would still have fun drinking and gossiping about the last four years while we shoved chips and salsa into our mouths.

I looked behind the old man to see a younger girl standing in line. Our eyes connected, and the aether tensed, giving me a glimpse of an unknown power. I gasped at the rawness of that power.

"I can help you, dear," Denise, the other teller working today, called.

I half listened to their conversation while I closed out the drawer. Something about an insurance payout. The voices never raised, but the tension in both was noticeable.

I carried the cash register drawer to the vault and signed it in before coming back out to see the young lady leave.

"Poor girl," Denise whispered as she opened her drawer to close it out.

"Who was that?"

Or better yet, *what was she?* The energy swarmed the bank. It fizzled, chaotically, but had this sharpness to it like it could be used at a moment's notice. I had never sensed anything like her with the aether.

"Kaity Herring. Her mother died two months ago. She's been in twice a week to check on the insurance money." Denise stopped to count her ones. "I don't know how she's living in that big house by herself. She's barely of legal age."

The empty revolving door spun again as the energy faded. Could Kaity be like me? Or something else entirely?

"Aren't you late?" Denise called from the vault as I watched the door stop.

I yelled my goodbye as I hurried out of the bank.

Fifteen minutes later, I rushed through the kitchen. I stopped short when I caught Dad's form standing at the stove. My fist clenched; tightness rose in my chest as I knew what this meant. *Dinner with Dad.* I took a breath before he turned to see me.

"Oh good. You're home." He smiled. "I made one of your favorites."

"I have plans with Grace."

The smell of pesto chicken pasta wafted throughout. Plans were about to be changed. How would I find out what happened with Luke if I couldn't meet with Grace tonight? I mean, Grace had messaged that he was okay, but I didn't really believe that. He lost his parents on his birthday. *How could anyone be okay with that?* I knew time would heal wounds, but was two years enough? Luke would still be hurting.

"Grace can wait," he said without meeting my gaze.

"But it's been a month since I've been home and I haven't spent any time with her yet," I whined; frustration slithered into my voice.

"Emma."

The inside of my mouth tasted metallic as I chewed the side of my cheek. Why couldn't he use my name?

"Ember," I said through clenched teeth but, like always, he ignored me.

He had agreed to use my birth name a month ago. He still wasn't honoring it.

"Grace can wait," he said, turning to look me in the eye. "I want to spend time with my daughter."

"That's all we've been doing for the last month.

Running, meditating, shooting every weekend." My voice grew louder as my arms swung out with each point.

"Em."

I turned toward him, arms midair, as he gave me a pointed look.

"You never minded all that stuff when you were younger."

That's because I didn't know any better.

"Dad, it's been a month, and with my schedule and hers, we haven't been able to see each other. It's been four years. Please? I can eat the leftovers tomorrow. I won't let them go to waste if that's what you're worried about."

He stepped forward as the pan sizzled in the background, no doubt burning to the bottom of the supposed stainless-steel coating.

"I'm not saying you can never see her, but you worked today and have an early morning tomorrow. Do you really want to stay out late knowing how bad you will feel in the morning?"

I opened my jaw to say *yes*. I didn't care, but a small flower magnet I'd made in grade school for Mom stared back at me. Stick to the plan. *Best behavior.* I needed my answers. I glanced back at Dad standing in the middle of the kitchen with his hands on his hips. His most natural pose.

"Okay," I muttered.

He nodded and immediately turned back to the stove, dismissing me once more.

I rushed out of the room into the foyer. Leaning back against the wall, I swallowed the taste of blood, gazing at the single photo of my mother taken from behind. Her head tilted in such a way that I could glimpse a smile on the barely visible corner of her lips. *Just breathe.*

How had she handled him? Had he been different with her? The picture gave me no answer as I hunched over, hands on my knees for support.

Fire, while wickedly cool to wield, was dangerous, and I took a long deep breath as I focused on pushing down the rising heat. But it wouldn't obey. I pushed the aether out. It snaked through the hall, confirming Dad still stood in the kitchen as I brought my hand up and, with it, released the buildup. A single flame danced on my palm, casting more light on the picture than the foyer ever contained.

I won't be here forever. I discharged the flame and darted upstairs to change out of work clothes. This house wouldn't become my prison again. I'd make it back to my newfound home—Berkeley. I didn't want to cut him out of my life, but what else could I do? It seemed he'd never accept another way. If he would talk to me or be willing to give me a small sign that he'd listen to my side, I wouldn't have to hide so much of my life from him. So far, he hadn't given me a spark of hope.

I tried to recall happier memories, but last month's grueling schedule popped up. Then high school and having to wake up at four in the morning every *damn* day. Years of sitting crossed-legged out on damp concrete. After a minute, I gave up. Most of the good ones were times with Luke and Grace. Later with Vanessa, her older brother Randy, and their cousin Evie.

Eventually, if Dad answered my questions, I would be able to leave. I had a future that included Lyra, Vanessa, and Evie. They were the long-lost sisters I didn't know I needed until I met them. But this time, I would keep in touch with Grace.

I was a different person with them, especially Lyra. She was the one person I could use my abilities around and not be worried she'd be disappointed in me. I had hoped to tell Grace tonight about everything. It was long overdue.

The last two years taught me that these powers I could control were not evil. That all the lectures and sermons Dad read to me didn't define me. There was a way to use my powers to help others. And once I found more people like me, I could show him that.

I opened my phone to see Grace with a margarita and a big smile on her face. She held the drink up to her pursed red lips. I laughed, then wiped away the escaped tear. How I missed her. Grace was optimistic growing up, and I could count on her to spin anything into a happier moment. Disappointed, I messaged Grace to let her know of the change of plans.

"Emma," Dad called from downstairs, and I headed down for one more normal dinner.

Four

EMBER

After watching Dad's favorite game show and his lame attempts to solve the puzzles, I headed back to my room. The fan spun a slow circle above me, barely lifting the stifling heat in the room. *Only a few more weeks of playing by the rules.*

The heat in the room rose. I'd be doing more than heating up the room if I didn't restrain my flame inside me. With a deep breath, I eyed the fan making its rounds. I closed my eyes. *Calm down and the heat will dissipate.* But the *shit* from today poured in.

I got up and opened the single window in the room. The cool breeze traveled up my arm, and I climbed out onto the middle of the roof. The rough shingles scraped against my skin as I lay back. The roof had been a sanctuary for me. I'd end up here after a long day of practice, school, and more practice when most of my classmates were at games or hanging out together.

It was silent moments like this that I thought about

Gran. I told myself the stars above would be the same stars that Gran saw. I hadn't seen her in thirteen years. I felt in my heart something bad must have happened to her. Why else would she visit each month until my eighth birthday and never again? She stayed long enough to read a bedtime story and tuck me in.

The twinkling lights reminded me of one story she told me multiple times.

Our people were once divided among thirteen tribes living across the plains until the Akkad came to wipe us out. The thirteenth tribe convinced the others to join together in order to beat back the enemy. Defeat was only a matter of time, but the people were not willing to give up. On the thirteenth day, their courage and strength were rewarded. Zodi, God of the Heavens, descended to bestow his elemental magic upon our people. That day the Akkad was destroyed. In honor of Zodi, our people renamed themselves Zodians.

I wiped the wetness from my cheeks. Gran stopped visiting after I drank the cure. Then we moved away under the cover of darkness.

That first taste of *salvation* bound my powers inside me. *Trapping them.* The wave of grief that overcame me confused and angered Dad. He spent that entire year reminding me *it was for the best.* Like it would be for the best if I took *it* a second time to rid myself of those powers once and for all. Was that the right choice after living without restraint for two years? Would my life be normal without the aether or connection to the fire? Would it give me the life I wanted? And did I know what life I wanted? *One where I didn't torch brand-new clothes or someone's eyebrows?*

A bright light engulfed me, and I squealed, rolling close to the edge of the roof. Grace appeared in the exact spot I was moments ago. *What the hell? How did she do that?*

"Grace?"

"Emma, are you okay?" A shout came through the opened window.

I turned toward the window, fists clenched, but Dad wasn't in the room. He must have been on the stairs.

"I'm fine." I listened to his steps fade before my eyes landed back on Grace. "What the hell?" I muttered.

She smiled. "I told you I had a lot to tell you." Her smile turned mischievous. "Why did you make me wait a whole month?"

This was the Grace I knew and missed these last few years. I wrapped my arms around her. Surprise dawned on her face before she hugged me back.

"Sorry. I tried."

"It's okay, but we need to chat now."

We perched on the roof, resting under the twinkling stars in silence. I remembered all those times we'd done this in our youth, giggling over boys.

I turned my head to her. "How did you do that?"

A smile grew on her face, and she sat back up, pivoting around with her legs crossed under her. "I have powers."

I copied her pose and whispered, "Powers, really?"

She rolled her eyes before nodding. "My great-great-

great-granddad was actually an angel. An angel that fell in love with a human and descended from Heaven." She took a breath and rushed the last bit. "It turns out that I inherited some of his abilities. My mentor told me I'm a Nephilim."

"A Nephilim?" *So, no secret boyfriend.*

"Yes. And look at this." She lifted her hand for me to see the new ring on her index finger. "My mentor said it's been in my family for over three hundred years."

The ring was silver, molded into wings with a rose-gold threaded through the wings to give it definition. Beautiful piece of jewelry, but bulkier than the usual style Grace wore.

"It looks great for being so old."

"Don't act like you don't know what I'm talking about," Grace said, crossing her arms.

"What?"

I'd never heard of a Nephilim before or angels really falling except from Sunday School. But I guess it made sense. I was a Zodian. Why couldn't there be Nephilim or others like that girl at the bank today?

"Ember," Grace said. "You're a Zodian. I'm a Nephilim, though I prefer the term half angel instead. Nephilim makes me sound like a frog or something." Her nose scrunched up.

I laughed. "Half angel makes little sense either, but yes, I'm Zodian."

"I knew it." Grace snapped her fingers. "My bosses told me you were, but I couldn't believe it at first. Why didn't you tell me?"

"I'm sorry I didn't tell you. I'd planned to tell you tonight." She gave me a pointed look. "I know, but the truth is that I wasn't supposed to get my powers back. It was an oops on Dad's part."

"Does he know?"

I shook my head. "No and he can't find out yet."

Her hands came to her hips. "I still can't believe I had to find out from my stuffy old bosses and not my best friend."

"I'm sorry. The times we did talk I felt awkward bringing up such a big issue."

"I get it. I've been busy these last couple of years, learning about everything." She stared up at the stars, a huge smile on her face. "This is awesome. My best friend and I are superheroes."

"I wouldn't go that far, Grace."

She grasped my hands. "But we are. You have powers and I have powers. I can shoot beams of light or, well, I should be able to. But I can go wherever I want with a simple thought. It's super cool except that Kaity has that power too."

"Kaity?" *Could it be the same girl from the bank?*

Grace's eyes widened before she answered. *Is she hiding another secret?*

"Yeah, Kaity Herring. She's a witch and can teleport as well. She's part of the gang." Grace turned to look at me. "Do you know her?"

I shook my head. "No. she came into the bank today and I felt"—*how to say this*—"the energy seemed to fizzle around her. Something different, but I couldn't figure out what."

Grace smiled. "That's her power."

A witch, the energy would be her unique signature.

"Em, don't you think you should tell your dad?"

I cringed. "I've thought about it, but I grew up with him telling me how bad supernaturals were," I said, and she waited. "I think it's for the best right now to not say anything at all."

"Your dad needs a reality check," Grace mumbled.

"I'm hoping to learn about my powers and their history. Other Zodians can help me with that if I could find out where they are."

I held my palm up to the sky, creating a fireball. I concentrated on the flame, and it grew to the size of a golf ball. The flame grew double in size. *Why would anyone want a normal life?* The fire flickered and dissipated.

Wide-eyed, Grace smiled. "My bosses said you were powerful, but I bet you're better than Kaity."

Who the hell are her bosses? "I doubt it." I caught her waiting look. "I mean, I'm an elemental, able to create and bend the elements, and you said Kaity is a witch. Can't a witch do more?" Like, well, she could teleport and I couldn't. Though, that would be a killer power.

"Fire Elemental is so cool," Grace whispered.

The little voice in the back of my head whispered *liar*.

"You can definitely help with the gang. This is a major game changer. Can you come tomorrow?"

"Angels are in gangs now?"

"Ember," Grace scoffed.

I turned back to Grace. "What gang?"

She frowned. "You didn't hear. Ugh okay. Luke and the others get together around ten or eleven every night before hitting the streets."

Why are they hitting the streets?

I must have looked confused because she continued. "They go out at night to kill the vampire population. It's been getting bad here in town. More people have gone missing or turned up dead in the last few years than in the last thirty."

"They kill vampires?" I laughed then wheezed. *Vampires were real.*

She sighed again. "I need to get going." She looked at her watch. "I'll explain tomorrow. Meet us at Parker Elementary at eleven." She stood.

"Grace, you know it depends on—" Before I could finish, a flash of light blinded me.

Gone. This was normal Grace. How many times in high school would I continue to chat on the phone after she already hung up? And I didn't even get a chance to ask her about Luke.

But before I could go inside, the aether stirred. A strange flutter started in the pit of my stomach. A vision. Luke standing in the ring. Sweat dripped from him as he surveyed his opponent. Eight rounds. No clear winner, and one more round to go. It only took one last shot to the jaw before his opponent crashed down to the mat.

I snapped out of the memory and trained my eyes on the woods that surrounded this suburb of Happy Valley.

While the woods didn't extend too far, they would eventually end at the shooting range. I took a deep breath as I pulled on the strings of the aether. The aether flowed along the roof into the grass. It hit the woods and came back to me. *Why did this sensation make me think of Luke?*

I couldn't see anything from the roof. The aether only gave signatures. While each creature was unique, similar beings left distinguishable traces, but this was something new. It didn't have the same feel as the wildlife that normally roamed the woods. I scooted to the edge of the roof, but before I could investigate, the presence was gone.

Five

EMBER

I sat crossed-legged on the dusty concrete floor of the range with twenty new candles spread out around me. I breathed. *In and out.*

"When you're calm, light all the candles at once." Lyra's voice came through the jimmy-rigged phone propped against a bench along the back.

Close enough to me that I could hear her instruction but far enough away that I wouldn't accidentally burn it. *Don't want to lose another.*

I sighed as the candles before me did nothing again. A breeze filtered through the pavilion; a small leaf landed on my knee. I placed it in my palm. A few seconds later, it floated above my hand before it dropped. *Lasted a bit longer this time around.*

"Kid, what are you doing?"

I rolled my eyes at Lyra's snarky attitude. "I don't understand why we're wasting time on lighting candles. I learned all this two years ago." I huffed. "I want to learn how to control the other elements."

A clicking sound came through the phone, and I could picture Lyra's hand on her hip as she made the sound with her tongue. "Light the damn candles."

Another minute passed before the tension in my shoulders eased and my breathing evened out. I visualized the candles lit and listened to my rhythmic heartbeat. The subtle breeze filtered through as the tall grass whistled. My eyes opened to find one unlit candle. *Damn, so close.*

"Well, did you do it?" Lyra's harsh voice filtered through.

I wanted to tell her I did, but I knew she would hear the lie. "There's one left."

"Close your eyes, and as you exhale, extinguish the candles."

I knew this would continue until all twenty candles were lit at the same time. For the last two years, I had been studying how to control the fire through meditation. *Something I hated with a passion.*

We argued for weeks about the next phase of training. Fire came naturally to me. It was the control I lacked. A fireball? *No problem.* A stream of fire shooting out of my hands. *Again, no problem.* The problem was that I could manipulate not one element but all of them. Aether, air, water, earth, and fire.

Aether developed faster than the rest of the elements. The aether allowed me to sense others. It was a light breeze winding its way between places and bringing back imagery of what it touched. It was overwhelming the first time it happened. I'd been sitting in a lecture hall with two hundred plus students. All the visions came in one after another. Piling on top of each other and suffocating me. I'd scrambled for the door. It was the only time Lyra had stepped foot on campus. She stayed two whole days with me in the dorm, teaching me how to control it. I ventured back out into the world when I could filter what the aether brought to me.

And then I'd spent the last couple of years learning about fire and how to control my emotions after the chem lab mishap. But the rest, *nada*. Water, earth, and air surfaced at times, but I couldn't really focus with them like fire. Zodians had one strongest element, and mine happened to be fire. But I didn't see any reason not to learn from the others. Lyra disagreed.

"Stop daydreaming."

The candles melted to tiny stubs at the harsh words. *Shit.*

"I'm sorry." I picked up my phone. "I lost focus." I closed my eyes. *In and out,* "I had no problem earlier this year. Are you sure we need to repeat this lesson?"

"Being home has brought up issues. Until you learn to push those aside and focus on your inner strength, we will not move on." I could hear her famous eye roll as she talked.

"Fine. I'll have to grab more candles for tomorrow's session."

"Tomorrow," she bit out as the line went dead.

I laid the phone back on the bench, but it binged. I opened up the text message from Grace.

Why didn't you come to the meeting?

I texted back *Dad* as a cop-out answer. I didn't know if I wanted to join a gang. That could put my plan in jeopardy. Throwing my phone into the bag, I scraped the candle wax off the concrete floor, then grabbed my equipment. I knew an archery session would put me in a better mood.

Hours later, I stopped by the local dollar store to buy more candles. The shelves sat empty as I eyed the section. At this rate, I would need to make my own candles. I'd wiped out their entire selection two days ago. I picked up the basket off the floor and headed to the front.

"Doug, how are you?" I asked, approaching the checkout counter.

Doug Davis graduated from high school one year after me and was dating Hannah Puecher. Hannah and Doug rounded out our group of friends back in the day. Hannah was a descendant of an American Indian, and it showed in her hickory skin, dark brown eyes, and coarse black hair. Our classmates thought I did as well since my skin had a permanent tan all year round, but I had violet eyes and thin black hair. Dad had never confirmed our

American Indian blood, which complicated senior year's ancestral project.

Doug looked up from a handheld device. "Oh hey, Em. Are you happy to be back in town? It was . . . what, four years?"

"Yep." I smiled, avoiding the first question.

"Not much has changed since you left. Hannah's excited to be working with you at the bank again. She couldn't stop talking the other night."

"Me too. I'm headed there now."

"Was there something you needed?" he asked and pointed to the empty basket.

I placed the basket with the others at the end of the checkout. "When will more candles come in?"

"I told Hannah you bought us out yesterday." He smiled at the new customer behind me.

I bit my lip. "I like that scent."

"You must light them all the time."

I edged closer to the door. "Yeah, when will you get more in stock?" I asked again, looking down at my watch to check the time. *I'm gonna be late.*

He typed one-handed on the computer in front of him. A second went by before Doug turned back toward me. "Ordered yesterday, but not sure if they will be on the truck today or in two days."

Dang. "Thank you!" I lifted my hand in a wave.

As I headed to my car, I glimpsed the local craft store, Jean Crafts. They could have candles.

I arrived late to my shift, but I purchased more

candles. My happiness outweighed the displeasure of my boss. Candles saved me from Lyra's wrath.

I stood behind the counter to wait on customers. The bank had busy moments and times where nothing happened. Hannah made the slow hours pass faster, but she had the day off.

The door chimed. The girl from the other day walked in, and the bank swarmed with the same energy. The hair on a customer changed from smooth to frizzy in seconds.

Kaity Herring.

Grace said she was a witch. She didn't look like a witch, but I guess I didn't look like a Zodian. Kaity's hair was strawberry blonde, framing her face while she wore faded jeans and a black tank top. The only jewelry was a pendant made of white topaz around her neck.

She stopped before my station. Her seafoam eyes met mine.

I smiled. "How can I help you?"

She looked around. "Is Denise here?"

"No, she had a morning shift. My name is Ember. May I help you?"

"Denise had been helping me with my mother's insurance."

Denise's comment from the previous day came back. "Maybe I can help. What is the account?"

"I'm Kaity, and my mother is Rachael Herring," she said as she pulled out a scrap of paper with an account written on it.

I typed the number and waited for the system to pull

up the information. All of the transactions seemed in order except no insurance money. "Were you waiting on insurance to come into the account?"

"I keep calling the insurance company, and they say they have deposited it into the account, but nothing has shown up that I can see."

Typing her mother's name into the system, I checked the records to see if another account existed. "There's another account." I clicked on the account, and sure enough, the insurance money sat there. "It looks like you're not on the account. You need to bring in documentation of your mother's death and the other account holder," I said, reciting bank procedure.

"The other account holder?" she asked.

Kaity leaned forward to see the screen, but with the privacy shield on, she couldn't read anything unless she stood directly in front of it.

I tried to remember if I could give out the other account holder's name. Behind me, the shift supervisor stood typing on a computer. I motioned to her, and she came around the desk.

I turned back to Kaity. "Hold on." I locked the screen and walked back to the supervisor. A brief discussion later, I stood in front of Kaity again. Her hands were behind her back as she waited. "The other account holder is Tom Herring."

"My dad." Her face scrunched up. "He's been dead for ten years."

I shrugged my shoulders. "He's on the account. You'll

need to bring in your birth certificate and both of the death certificates. That should be enough proof for the manager to move the funds into your account."

"Oh my gosh, thank you!" She clapped her hands together, a smile on her face. "This has been more helpful than my last three visits with Denise."

I smiled, glad that I could help her even if I couldn't light silly candles. From the sound of the situation, she needed help. "You're welcome."

The aroma of cheese attacked me as I walked into the house. My favorite pizza sat on the counter. A medium buttery crust with mozzarella cheese, pepperoni, American cheese, and ham. I grabbed a paper plate and several slices, and I turned to the living room, where the sound of Dad's favorite show played. He sat in his chair, munching on a slice.

I took a bite before saying hello. "Thanks for getting pizza tonight. It's been ages since I had it."

He grinned but turned back to the puzzle to attempt an answer. I laughed at his poor guess before devouring the rest of my slice. A smile plastered on my face as I glanced around the room.

My shoulders sagged, and a sigh escaped. I looked down at my empty plate. Heaviness set in as I thought about this so-called *future*.

Has this always been Dad's plan? I sometimes

wondered late at night if he sent me to Berkeley to end my relationship with Luke. Maybe it wasn't really about my safety or Luke's but what Dad wanted.

He turned to me with a smile on his face. "What's wrong?" he asked, concern flickered in his eyes.

"Nothing, I had a long day."

He nodded as I grabbed our empty plates and headed to the kitchen. I walked out of view and leaned against the fridge. The cool doors offered a slight chill as I controlled my breathing. I knew when I stepped back into the living room, I would ask Dad about Mom.

Once my fire was in check, I headed back, thankful the show played the ending credits. He would have to give me his full attention. I stood against one of the two pillars that separated the open floor plan of the living room and dining room.

"Emma, I figured you were heading to bed."

My hand clenched at my side, but getting angry right now would not help my cause.

His gaze shot to my hands. "I'm sorry, Em. It's so natural to me. You'll always be my little Emma."

He stood to walk out of the room.

"Dad," I whispered when he brushed past me. "I need to know more about my mother. You don't ever talk about her. Can we please sit down and chat?"

His left eye twitched, his spider veins more prominent than normal. "There's nothing to say. She's not here anymore, sweetheart. Knowing her will make you miss her more."

I didn't agree. "Please. I know absolutely nothing.

Where did she grow up? How did you meet?" I fired off questions at him. He couldn't possibly know what it was like to not have a mother around. He had Grandma Sue. I needed some kind of closure. I needed to know that she loved me. That she wanted me. That if she hadn't died, she would have chosen *me* as I was.

"I," he started, then his gaze shifted to the hallway beyond where the single picture of my mother hung.

A picture of both of them in the bed of a pickup truck. Their backs to the camera. My mother half turned, looking at Dad. A smile on her delicate face. A half face. *Not enough.* The sun shone down on them, distorting her coloring, but with Dad's pale skin and my perpetual tan, I knew the coloring came from her. Did we have the same eyes? While it wouldn't help me learn to control my flames, one goddam picture of my mother with her actually looking at the camera wouldn't hurt.

He looked back at me, hurt in his eyes. "You look exactly like your mother." He smiled. "Optimistic. She was excited to have you. The love she had for you when you were born poured out of her as she cradled you."

Yes. The only piece I knew for certain was that she had died several months after my birth.

"Thank you," I whispered to him. His smile encouraged me. "Do you know where she grew up? Gran only told me stories of ancient warriors for bedtime."

He stiffened beside me before he took in a deep breath. "Forget that side. You're my daughter, and that's what matters right now." Sensing the tension in my body, he pressed his fingers into my shoulder before continuing. "Serafina left and decided to never visit you again. It's been years. Nothing good comes from learning about something you have no control over."

I sidestepped; his hand dropped off my shoulder. "I don't understand. It's my choice. I want to know. She's part of me. She named me Ember. Could that be a family name?"

Why did this have to be hard? Other families discussed their lost loved ones regularly. Why couldn't we?

I held his gaze and knew he would tell me no more tonight. As wetness spilled down my cheeks, I pivoted toward the stairs. When I reached the landing, I heard him at the bottom.

"Good night," he called. Then quieter, "It's for your own good."

I stood on the top step as tears tried to cleanse my soul. My own good? How could he be the judge of that? When my breathing slowed, I ventured to my room, but the walls suffocated me. The faded pink paint constricted me.

I yanked the window up, but it stuck halfway. The hole was big enough that I climbed through to the roof. Unlike Grace's last visit, I planned to leave. It had been years since the last time I climbed down the side of the house. But once learned, it wasn't hard to remember the skill.

While a jump wouldn't kill me, I feared a sprained ankle. I sat on the edge of the roof, twisted onto my belly, and slowly lowered myself until my foot touched the dining room's windowsill. When my foot connected with solid wood, I pushed off and jumped the rest of the way down. I landed in a crouch.

Crickets greeted me.

With no destination in mind, I headed off down the street. My mind replayed the conversation again. Why couldn't he talk to me? What was he hiding?

A large stone lay in front of me, and I took my anger out on it. The rock skidded to a stop farther down the street in front of Luke's house. When did I turn down his street? The house rested like a tomb.

Why did others decide what I needed to know? Why did no one call when Luke got hurt? Had Grace really thought I didn't want to know because I left town and left them all behind? I hadn't been the one to stop replying to messages. I'd only quit trying when I received nothing for months.

My eyes closed, and I stood in the night's silence with a deep breath in and a slow breath out. My feelings for Luke were complicated. He'd gotten me to see a different world. He'd taken the time to coax me out of the sheltered life Dad built around me. Many firsts had happened with him.

Gravel crunched behind me.

I turned, bringing forth my hands, palms opened, facing the unknown threat.

A man stood a few feet from me, his clothes dark, his smile darker as he stared at me. His face screamed botched Botox procedure.

"She looks like the other one," he said.

The other one? What did he mean? I slid one foot back and bent my knees a little as I stared at the odd man. His pale skin gleamed under the streetlamp.

"I'll seize her, Titan," a voice beside me said.

Crap. He'd been talking to his partner. He stood off in a neighbor's front yard, another dark smile on his face. There was something wrong with these two. The aether that swirled around them reminded me of the time Grace, Hannah, and I found a dead opossum in the backyard. It'd been there for days, and the smell alone sent us away.

They were trouble. *I need to leave.*

I glanced back toward Luke's house, to safety, but seconds later, it hit me again. No one would be there to help. Death had taken them. The distraction cost me as the two men disappeared from where they were.

"What the fuck?" I said to no one, but the aether fizzled as the figures appeared on each side of me.

One grabbed me around the upper body, pulling me back.

"Let me go!"

Locking my arms, I tried to pry their arms off by slamming mine straight up, but they were too strong. He dragged me back as I watched Luke's house get farther and farther away.

"Now, now, let's not hurt your pretty face," the man I thought was Titan whispered behind me.

I shivered at his frigid breath. His body, cold to the touch, seemed at odds in the August heat.

"Leave me alone," I yelled as they heaved me down the road.

I struggled, trying to free my hands that they had pinned to my side. I kicked at his knees, and when that didn't work, I swung my leg as fast as I could and nailed his groin.

He groaned, tossing me down.

I landed on my knees, pushing my palms into the gravel. The sharp rocks cut into my skin, and it seemed like a ton of bricks laid against my chest as I tried to draw in air. When I caught my breath, I dashed away back down the street toward Luke's house. The other guy stepped in front of me, but I didn't stop. I brought forth my palms and swung, making him take several steps back. He threw a punch. I blocked it with my arm as I brought my knee up. Kicking fast, I connected with his groin. He doubled over as the first one had. Smirking, I sprinted around him before a hand grabbed to pull me back. The loose gravel under my feet shifted, and I landed hard on my ass.

The dark, sinister creep stood above me. "Let's get her in the van," he screamed at his colleague, still groaning on the ground.

I could see a white utility van parked at the end of the street. If they got me into it, would I be able to free myself? I couldn't risk it. I summoned fire to the tip of my fingers, ready to attack.

"Leave!"

A familiar deep voice spoke from behind me. Luke's boxing match filtered through my mind again. The determination in his eyes as he slammed another win filled me with that same pride I had years ago.

The guy standing over me sprang at the newcomer while his partner was still groaning on the ground.

I turned toward him. *Luke.* He stood tall under the yellow streetlamp. His bicep strained against the sleeve of his black T-shirt as he swung at the oncoming assailant.

I must have whispered his name, for he turned to stare at me through his displaced locks of caramel hair. His eyes widened when they met mine. That cost him as the guy sent an uppercut to his jaw.

"Luke," I yelled and tried to stand but tripped over Titan.

Luke moved faster than I could track, but the aether told me he was still there. Before I knew it, Luke held a pointed wooden stake against the chest of his attacker. With one smooth move, he thrust it straight into the guy's heart. That's when the screaming started.

What the hell? I gasped as the man disintegrated into dust before my eyes. *Vampire?*

I placed my palms against the ground to push myself up. I watched as gravel scattered around the now deserted road except for Luke and me.

He appeared to be the same boy I used to know. His piercing copper eyes locked onto mine. He'd been tall in high school, but it seemed he sprouted again. My head would lay against his chest. *Perfectly.* He stared at me. Almost in disbelief that I was standing there before him.

I stepped slowly toward him, trying not to frighten

him away. Not before I touched him to make sure he was real.

"Luke."

But his eyes flashed down, and he hissed. I caught the glint of his white teeth before he closed his mouth. Sharp, pointy teeth. A vampire's teeth.

Grace said he was okay.

"Luke," I said again, rubbing my hands against the back of my shirt.

"Please don't, Em," he murmured, turning his head to the side, breaking eye contact with me.

I stepped back, unsure what to do. A vampire stood in front of me, but this was Luke.

Memories of my gran's bedtime stories filtered through my mind. The subtle warnings she would carve through the stories made sense. I knew Dad had sheltered me. What if Mom had survived? Would I have been part of this world sooner?

I glanced behind him, his house. The pale-blue siding mourning in the moonlight. "I'm sorry for your loss."

He looked at me, his eyes haunted. Behind there lay a secret. I took a step closer, knowing I would always be safe with him.

"How did it happen?" I asked, cursing myself for discussing such a sore topic. "No, I'm sorry. That was insensitive. Don't answer that. I'm truly sorry, Luke."

He stepped into the moonlight, closer. "Don't act like you care." He spoke low but firm.

I closed my eyes. "I do care, Luke." I took another step.

The distance between us narrowed. "You don't get to care. Not when you left the way you did four years ago."

I flinched at his words, the harsh underlying truth. "I'm sorry. I should have talked to you before I left."

He half turned. "It wouldn't have made a difference. You chose to follow what your dad laid out for you instead of following your heart."

We stood in the middle of the road, his eyes locked on his parents' house and mine on his. I wanted to share with him what I learned from leaving all those years ago, but I didn't think he would appreciate the reminder that I hadn't chosen him.

The memory flooded my senses. I could smell the perfume I had deemed appropriate for a wedding in the slight breeze. I stood in the courthouse's hallway after exiting the elevator, only to run into Dad. He stood waiting for me.

"You can't be serious?" he asked. "What will happen when he finds out who you are? That could put him in danger." Dad spoke clearly and slowly.

Those words sent me back out to my car. I left that minute for Berkeley, a plan he had prepared in advance. Happy I'd chosen his way. But did I?

"Em."

I looked at Luke, his copper eyes holding a touch of sadness in them. "How did this happen?"

He glanced away toward his house again.

"Grace said you were okay." I placed my hand into his.

His warmth hit me as his pulse raced. Different from the other two.

"You should head home, Em." He stepped away and my hand fell.

"Luke."

He shook his head and disappeared into the night. I wanted to understand, but maybe I didn't have that right.

Six

EMBER

I yawned and pulled the door to Jean Crafts once more. It didn't budge, but the time printed said it opened at nine. *Fuck.* Guess I shouldn't have tried to light all the candles I'd bought the day before. Now I had none for today's session with Lyra.

I checked the time once more before I walked back to the bank to start my shift. At least today, Hannah worked with me. I smiled at her. She glanced around, making sure the manager was in the back before she moved over to me.

"Did you hear?" she whispered.

"No."

She leaned in even closer. "Jean's missing."

"Missing?" No wonder the shop had been closed.

Hannah nodded. "She lives a few houses down from us and the sheriff . . ." She rolled her eyes. "The dick would tell anyone close enough that she ran off."

"Jean?" That made little sense. She was part of the

town. She married, raised her kids here, and cultivated a shop all the stay-at-home moms loved. "Why would he say that?"

Hannah shrugged her shoulders as a customer came in, and we had to break apart. A few minutes later, we ventured back together.

"The sheriff thinks anyone who isn't white 'ain't worth the time,'" Hannah said in a harsh whisper.

"I thought Smith was sheriff?"

Hannah shook her head again. "Nah, this asshole got elected last round."

I looked at Hannah's dark skin and black hair and sighed at the injustice that still plagued this town. I saw it at Berkeley, but not as often as I had while living here with Dad. He was as white as one could be, raising his tanned little girl. He claimed I stayed outside too long in the summer sun. Though, from their looks, they knew the truth.

"Is this a bad time?" a voice inquired on the other side of the window.

Hannah and I both looked at the same time. Her jaw dropped open and then closed.

"Christo?"

"Oh hey," he said, "it's Em, right?"

He remembered my name. The other girls in the dorm called him a six-foot-three sexy god. Soft blonde waves curled around his ears, framing his strong jawline. Days-old stubble enhanced his rugged but refined appearance. His blue eyes seemed trained on me as his smile widened.

A giggle escaped Hannah.

I ignored her and asked, "What are you doing in Happy Valley?"

"I'm passing through on my way home from a meeting."

"I see." We stood there for a second. "Is there something I can help you with?"

Hannah gazed at him with googly eyes. I nudged her back in the direction of her counter, but she didn't budge.

Christo's pearly smile hit us full blast, and Hannah choked on her titter. I patted her back until she sounded more normal.

Christo waited a bit longer before saying, "I tried the ATM outside, but there was an error."

"Oh, okay," I said as Hannah blushed and practically shoved me through the swinging half door.

"Why don't you go out there and see if *you* can help." Hannah's voice came out raspy.

I rolled my eyes at her, then nodded to Christo, and he turned around to head out. I glanced at Hannah, and she mouthed *holy hell, he's on my list* before I caught up with him at the door. He nodded and motioned for me to go first through the rotating door.

He followed seconds later when the revolving door decided to be the problem and came to a complete stop. Christo bumped into my backside. His hot breath tickled my neck. I shivered as I tried to get the door to start again. The glass window fogged as he added his weight to the door. His complete form pressed against me. The door squeaked and released us.

Outside, Christo led the way to the ATM. He turned

to smile at me, and I slid my eyes to the machine. The screen appeared normal.

"Why don't you try again?" I said as I stood beside it. He nodded. A few minutes later, cash ejected from the bottom. "Awesome! So glad it's not broken."

"Thank you, Em."

I smiled at him, thinking back to when we lived in the same dorm that year in college. He'd been the *it* guy in the dorm, and many of the girls had left his room in the wee hours.

"Would you like to get dinner?" He asked as we crossed back over to the side door.

"Um," I started. *Why the hell not? You need to move on, plus none of those girls had ever complained.* "When?"

He laughed like he read my thoughts.

"I'll be back in two weeks."

I nodded, and we exchanged numbers.

Hannah squealed when I came back into the bank. "Did you get his number?"

"Yes."

"What's that look on your face?"

I glanced around the empty room. "It's kind of nice to be out there again."

I hadn't dated too many people in high school due to my grueling schedule and well, Dad, but when I left for college, I'd been too heartbroken that first year to even think about dating anyone else. As my broken heart mended that second year, I enjoyed going out on the town with my roommate and her family. By the time I thought about dating, I had another reason not to.

The bully from Chem 101 and the seared smell of his eyebrows, burnt to a crisp, flashed through my mind. At least he got my point.

"He's damn sexy and is going on my cheat list." Hannah had a wide smile on her face. She paused for a moment. "Was he your first crush after Luke?"

My cheeks heated again as green eyes flashed before my eyes. I hadn't thought of them in two years as my world exploded the same night that I'd met that mysterious guy. All dressed in black. I'd been too drunk to get his number.

"Oh my, you're blushing. Did you ask him out?"

I put the picture out of my mind and answered Hannah's last question. "He asked me out."

"Tell me everything." Hannah squealed again.

I leaned onto the counter. "And you don't even have a cheat list because you'll never cheat on Doug."

She paused for a moment. "You're no fun. Can't I just imagine that sexy god ripping into me?" Laughing, she pulled me into a hug, jumping up and down, singing "you have a date" over and over.

"Excuse me."

I released Hannah. "Hello." I smiled, still affected by Christo's offer and Hannah's enthusiasm.

"If you're done chatting with your friend."

My eyes narrowed at the rude guy in front of me. *Why were hot guys so rude?* Even in this autumn heat, he wore dark wash jeans with a black fitted coat over a simple black tee. *It fit too tight, cutting the circulation to his brain.* And those annoying curls peeked out over the shirt.

"I'm sorry, sir." Irritation heated my insides as I shot him a faux grin. His lips went from full and *kissable* to a thin line. *Good.* He knows I'm pissed. "How can I help you?"

We stared at each other for a full minute, determined not to let the other win.

He blinked, and his eyes held a look of bewilderment for a second.

"Can I help you?" I asked, smirking as I'd won the imaginary staring contest.

He cleared his throat, eyes darting away from mine. "I was wondering about opening a checking account." He scanned the deserted lobby.

I glanced at Hannah, and she rolled her shoulders before I looked back. "There are brochures over at that table." I pointed to the center of the room where a round cherry wood table sat. Stacked on top were clear plastic containers holding pamphlets.

He turned in that direction. "Which one?" he called over his shoulder.

I sighed and stomped over to show him. I plucked out the brochure and handed it to him. "Here."

He bumped my hand instead. Electricity ran down my arm, and I dropped the paper.

"Sorry, static shock." He laughed, bending over to pick up the paper.

Static shock. His green eyes lit his entire face. My

body responded to his laugh, my lips curved to mirror his. Why was I having major déjà vu? I took a deep breath, and why was I just standing there? He didn't need me for anything else. *Ripping.* Hannah's earlier statement echoed. I shook my head and turned to leave.

"Thanks," he mumbled and glanced around the lobby again before dashing out of the side door.

I stopped in my tracks and watched him leave, almost sad to see him go, but that sounded crazy. He'd been rude and killed the vibe after Christo left.

Hannah stood beside my station. "That guy was rude." Her eyes widened. "But downright handsome too. I wonder who's hotter?"

Rude Guy? "Christo," I said a little too fast.

Her smile widened more, and for the rest of our shift, we talked about Berkeley and boys.

Seven

EMBER

I sat cross-legged on the cold concrete floor with candles in front of me, waiting for Lyra to answer the phone. I had lit all three candles before I made the call. Maybe it would help to clear my mind of last night's attack, Christo coming into the bank along with that jerk, and seeing proof that vampires were real. Especially the fact that vampires were real and Luke was one. It unnerved me that I hadn't really taken Gran's stories as truth but more of a Hans Christian Andersen tale.

"Ember." Her voice echoed throughout the pavilion. "Did you hear what I said?"

My mind blanked, and I sighed, "No, sorry."

"What's gotten into you? Clear your mind."

I closed my eyes. "Lyra." I took a deep breath and another. "I'm ready for your wisdom."

"Your sarcasm won't get you anywhere." She sputtered, her voice chopped in and out.

I opened my eyes to look at the phone, which had lost the signal. "Lyra, are you there?"

"Of course. Let's light the twenty candles all at once this time."

I cringed. "I could only get three."

"Three candles?" she questioned. "You better be able to light three damn candles."

I leaned back on my palms, wincing at the pain. The memory of the night before flashed again like a movie in my mind.

I stood. Movement helped me think. After Luke saved me, all I thought about as I drifted off to sleep was the fact that Luke wasn't okay like Grace had said. It twisted my stomach into knots. Luke was a vampire. The long, elongated teeth and disappearing act, that was not okay.

I paced a few rounds before speaking again. "Last night I took a late walk."

"And why is that relevant?"

"Vampires tried to carry me off, but my ex saved me before they could."

"Ember." Lyra's voice strained. "Why didn't you use your powers?"

I paused at her question. "I didn't think to use them until much later, then Luke was there."

"Luke?"

"You know the ex-boyfriend that I left when I went to college."

Lyra made a sound, but I couldn't understand what

she said. She heard about Luke enough that first year we met.

"The moment they showed, I thought they were normal humans, and how many times have I heard not to reveal my powers to the public?"

She huffed, "If it comes down to your safety, use your powers. Your strongest element is fire. That would scare off normal humans, and it's doubtful they would have talked about it to anyone. And since they were vampires, they would have left very quickly." She laughed as if she made a joke.

I looked at my phone lying on the concrete. "It just didn't occur to me," I repeated.

"Then we will start. But first, remember that you need to limit how much power you use at once."

I sat down and plucked my phone from the stone bench. "How come we've never discussed this before?"

Why didn't this come up in the last two years? Why did I always feel like she held back information?

"You weren't ready. You didn't want to acknowledge what really went bump in the night." She blew into the phone. "You wanted to know how to manage it. How to make sure it didn't surface at the wrong times."

"Yes, but isn't learning the limitations going along with that?"

"You can't light candles half the time, especially now that you decided it was time to go home and confront your dad. All the work you've done is unraveling every minute you waver over your choice. Choose and we can move on."

"That's not fair. It's my future to decide!" I yelled.

My pulse quickened as the anger rose. I took a deep breath.

"That right there." Her voice came through clear and crisp, breaking my concentration. "When you get angry, you immediately calm yourself. You want to know why we're back to basics. This is it. Give in to the anger. It's a part of you. Embrace yourself. Embrace the chaos."

I sat there. Anger was trouble. The main reason Dad taught me archery. Patience and calm rewarded the archer, not anger and thoughtlessness.

"Ember, Zodians were warriors long before they received their powers. They used their anger to fuel their strength and not dominate how they acted. Trust your instincts."

I said nothing as I processed what she said. It sounded doable, but could I work through my anger?

"Now, I want you to shoot your bow and light the three candles the moment the arrow leaves the strings," she said. "Are you moving?"

I climbed to my feet and picked the bow off the stone table where I had left it earlier. I stepped off the edge of the concrete where the sand and grass met the pavilion. I relaxed my muscles.

"Aim for the farthest target."

Visualizing, I saw the candles lit and the arrow dead center. I took a deep breath. I pulled the string tight, energy flowed into me, resonated against my skin, raising the hair on my arms. I released my arrow.

"Well? You remember I can't see what you're doing?"

I turned to see the three candles lit. *I did it.*

"Ember, come on."

"Yes, they're lit."

"And the arrow?" Lyra said.

I turned back around to look at the arrow. "It's dead center."

"Now, how did you do it?" she asked.

"I don't know."

She sighed before continuing, "You didn't focus your full attention. You let your body do it for you. I know you think you can't do this, but Ember, this is your blood. It's in your DNA. Lighting candles is basic. You can do much more if you just stop overthinking. The flames will do whatever you want them to do. They are yours to master."

I said nothing for a while. I wanted to reflect on what she said, but time wasn't on my side.

"Ember, someone's coming."

I turned toward the gravel road. How did she know? I heard crunching coming toward me. I gathered up the candles from the floor, shoving them into my bag before picking up my phone.

An SUV came into view around the last corner. Black with a logo on the side. While I couldn't see the logo yet, I knew what it said. Dad would be here any minute.

"Who is it?" Lyra said.

"It's my dad. I'll call you back later."

"Repeat that exercise as often as possible, and I'll let you know when I'm available next."

I said goodbye and slipped the phone into my back pocket. After two years of training under Lyra, I didn't know what she did for a living. Heck, I wasn't even sure she was a Zodian.

"Hey, sweetheart," Dad called through the open window.

I stepped off the concrete to greet him.

He climbed out. "I wanted to apologize about last night. I realized my mistake." He came over to me and embraced me. "I loved your mother so much. It's hard to talk about her."

"I understand, Dad. I do. I loved her too, and I didn't know her."

He smiled at me. "She was a beautiful woman, both in form and spirit." He motioned to one of the stone benches. "I met her in South Dakota on a Native American reservation."

"What were you doing there?"

He hesitated a moment before responding, "I worked for my parents collecting antiquities. I'd tracked a lead on an ancient sword belonging to a Shaman, but I never made it. Makani blindsided me."

I smiled at him, pictured him and her walking past each other only to stop and turn back to smile.

"She saw the sword I carried and boldly stated it belonged to her family. That I'd stolen it." He laughed, reaching his arm around me. "I stared at her and said to prove it."

"How did she prove it?" I asked.

His eyes lit up as the memory came to him. I had never seen Dad this lighthearted before.

"She asked for the sword. When I gave it to her, she gripped the helm and split the sword into two short swords. I had seen nothing like it before. When she gave the sword back to me in one piece, I tried to replicate what she had done but couldn't."

"Did you give her the sword?"

Sadness pooled in his eyes. "No. The sword belonged to my family, so I couldn't. She gave me her number and told me to call her when I passed through Vegas."

"Vegas?"

"One of the many places she lived before she moved in with me." He turned to look at me. "I stopped, and we grew a friendship into love."

I hugged him and buried my face in his shoulder. "Sorry. I know you lost someone too, but it's so hard not to know anything about her."

"Shh, it's okay. I need to talk about her more," he whispered into my ear. I nodded as my tears soaked into his shirt. "I knew her for such a short time but miss her more each day."

"Thank you for telling me this. Maybe tonight after supper we can chat some more."

"I need to get back to work." He nodded before leaving.

"See you later."

Eight

EMBER

On my next day off, I sat in a corner booth at Eats!, one of my favorite local restaurants, waiting for Grace. The cool temperature inside chilled my sweat-damped arms. I'd been out at the range practicing lighting the candles I'd bought yesterday.

"Hey girl, hey," Grace yelled as she climbed into the opposite seat.

I bumped my head against the back of the booth. "Ouch," I whispered to myself, looking at Grace.

"Oh, that looked like it hurt." She smiled at me before turning to look around the eatery.

Rubbing my head, I turned with her.

"Do you see that red-haired guy there?" Grace asked.

The redhead in question sat four tables from us with a group of six. They were laughing at something someone had said. The redhead at the table leaned back against his chair, lifting the front two legs off the ground.

"Yes"

"That's Jason, I've been trying to get him to notice me for weeks now."

"Man, he must have a protection spell against your charms if you haven't caught him yet," I said back to Grace. I'd never known her not to get the guy.

She gave me a smug smile, her eyes twinkling in the low lighting of the restaurant.

"What can I get you guys to eat?" The waitress came over to our table, blocking my view of the hottie redhead.

I grabbed a menu from the waitress and looked at the new items listed. After the waitress left with our order, I looked back at Grace. "So why did you want to meet?" And then I lowered my voice. "And you told me Luke was okay."

Her eyebrow lifted. "He is."

I lowered my voice even more. "He's a vampire. I saw the fangs."

Grace leaned down against the table to meet my eyes. "I thought I told you."

Typical Grace. "But is he okay?" I asked again.

She rolled her eyes. "Yes, he's fine. The gang is meeting tonight around eleven, and it might be nice for you to join them."

I leaned cautiously back in my seat. I already had a run-in with Luke, and he didn't seem like he wanted me anywhere near him. "Does Luke want me to come?"

Her head tilted to the side; I could see that she hadn't expected the question. "Um," she started, "he didn't ask for you to come, but with your powers, I think it would be a good idea."

"You know I didn't agree to hunt vampires in the night." I kept my voice low, but the table next to us turned to look at me. I smiled at the older couple before turning back to Grace.

"Ember with your abilities—"

I cut her off. "Keep your voice down," I said in a near whisper.

She rolled her eyes at me. "Em, with your abilities, you could help a ton in the field."

I looked over to see the waitress headed in our direction, my toasted pesto chicken sandwich on its way. I opened my mouth, but the sweet aroma of baguettes hit my nostrils.

Once the waitress refilled our water glasses and headed back to the kitchen, I answered Grace. "You know I don't have complete control of my powers yet, and I've never used them in a fight before."

I picked up half of my sandwich. I glanced at Grace when she didn't answer and laughed. She had taken a bite of her grilled five-cheese sandwich. Strings of melted goodness hung down her chin. I turned back to my sandwich. There would be plenty of time to talk later.

Fifteen minutes later, we piled our plates on top of each other at the edge of the table. I leaned back in my seat, thinking I'd ruined my appetite for supper.

"Em, vampires are invading our town." She leaned against the table. "Vampires are picking off the people stupid enough to venture out at night. There are only four of us that can fight, and we all can't go out every night."

"I'm not convinced I would be any help. What if I'm more of a liability?"

"Luke, Kaity, Ted, and Nathan need backup. You would be extremely helpful." She leaned closer to me. "Vampires don't like fire."

Her lame attempt to convince me brought forth a smile. "I'll think about it," I said at last.

She lifted her hands and squealed, drawing attention from the same couple as before.

"But I'm not promising anything." I leaned closer to her. "Do you know anything about Jean?"

Grace scooted closer. "Sheriff thinks she's run off, but Luke thinks a vamp got her."

A vampire got Jean?

Grace continued, "That's why they need you." She nodded to confirm her statement, then smiled at me. With her bill in hand, she stood. "I'll catch you later." She gave me a salute, headed off, and threw over her shoulder, "Think about it. See ya tonight."

I watched her pay and smile at me before skipping out the door. Light flared at the edge of the alley as she entered and disappeared.

If I went to the meeting, what would I be agreeing to join? A group of what, what were they? Hunters? Supernatural killers? Vampire Slayers? Dad would disown me if I joined them.

"Why does my life have to be so complicated?" I muttered.

The last thing I need to join is a vampire hunting squad.

A short five-block drive from my house, I parked on the side of the elementary school. The summer night made instant sweat on the back of my neck. A few vehicles were parked out front in the circle drive, but on the side closest to the play yard, I stood alone. Not knowing where to enter, I headed to the front doors.

I pulled on the doors and grunted. *Locked.* I stepped back to see if there were any signs of life inside the school. No light showed through the first-floor windows. If I remembered correctly, Parker Elementary closed after I graduated from fifth grade. Why had they chosen this place? I trekked back around to try the lunchroom door.

This one came open with little effort. The smack against the outside wall made me cringe. Now everyone would know I was here. *Late.* I walked into the room after pulling the door closed.

"Thanks for joining us."

I turned. Luke leaned against the lunch line with a glass in his hand. I tried to determine the color of the liquid in the dimly lit lunchroom, but he gulped down the rest while he waited for me to answer him. *Was he drinking blood?*

"I know you," a voice said from the opposite side of the room.

I turned to see Grace beside a redhead. The girl from the bank. Kaity Herring. I lifted my hand, waving as I noticed that Ted and his cousin Nathan sat at the same table. Ted went to school with Grace, Luke, and me. He'd spent most of his time on his laptop, and it seemed nothing changed. A laptop sat in front of him now. Luke and Ted had been best friends since birth. It had sometimes made me think I was the third wheel. Nathan, on the other hand, was Ted's younger cousin. He'd been the baby of our group, hanging out for a few adventures during senior year when he'd been a freshman.

"Let's start." Luke walked over to the group.

I headed in that direction until a movement caught my eye.

Luke glanced back at my frozen frame. "Ignore Bob, he's the bartender."

"Bartender?" I asked, looking at the person behind the lunch counter.

Not human? He had reddish skin that couldn't be natural and small horns coming out of his head. They curved around his skull and were a deep maroon color barely visible in the heap of chestnut curls.

"Em, this is a bar for demons or whoever else wants a drink. A sanctuary," Luke clarified.

I eyed Grace, and she shrugged her shoulders. *She could have told me what to expect.* I had envisioned them in the dark, covered in cobwebs with flashlights. What I found was a clean lunch room, almost exactly the same as when I was a kid here. The only difference was the stack of liquor behind the counter and the occupants in the room.

I took a seat beside Grace. The anxiety had built and induced the flames within. I'd managed to skip dinner with Dad, claiming a stomach ache, which was normal. *Normal life this or normal life that.* The only phrases out of Dad's mouth this month.

Luke called out to the group, "Let's get started. Everyone knows Em."

Great introduction. Ted and Nathan nodded. Kaity, who I technically hadn't met, gave me a smile before turning back to Luke. Her smile extended when it landed on him.

"The vampires are getting cocky. They tried to kidnap her a couple of nights ago."

Grace grabbed my arm, and I patted her hand, murmuring soothing words to her. Our eyes locked, and I promised to tell her later.

"They've successfully taken Jean."

"Are we sure it was them? The sheriff said she ran off," Ted asked.

"Yes," I said. "The vampires that tried to take me mentioned that I looked like the other one, meaning Jean, I'm assuming. We both have that dark skin and dark hair combination."

Luke nodded. "I agree. Jean likes to take late-night walks. I've seen her a few times this summer. I believe they captured her like the others."

My head snapped up. "Others?" The vampires had taken more?

Luke made eye contact before answering. "Yes, there have been . . ."

"Eight in the last twelve weeks," Kaity piped in.

"All with dark hair and skin," Ted said.

I sat and listened to Luke list the vampire nests he'd found in the area. He figured the missing girls would be there if they were alive.

"Okay, let's split into teams and see if we can end any vamps tonight," Nathan yelled, pumping his fist in the air, always the most enthusiastic of the group.

Seemed he'd not changed much either. I laughed, then swallowed the lump in my throat, realizing I'd missed them these last years.

Everyone started to head toward the door. *Do I have what it takes to fight with them?* Dad's face came into focus.

"I'm not going," I blurted. "I've never been in a fight. Dad only taught me basic self-defense."

"But you have powers? Grace says you're powerful," Kaity asked.

Grace gave me a sheepish look as I rolled my eyes and tightened my grip on the cross-body purse strap. "Well, not sure how powerful, but yes, I can make some fireballs. Though I've never fought with them or even thought about it." I glanced at Luke, his jaw locked as he looked at me. The disappointment in his eyes reflected the same hurt look from last night before he vanished in the dark. "I'm sorry."

His eyebrows drew closer as a slight nod occurred. "Come by tomorrow, and we can go over the basics and see what you need to work on," Luke said, breaking the connection.

I opened my mouth. *I can't do that.*

Ted hollered, "Let's move out," and they filed out.

Grace gave me a half hug. "I'll let you know if they find any of the missing girls."

A light flashed, and she disappeared. I stood in the cafeteria alone.

"You want a drink?" a low voice asked.

I jumped at the sound of the demon bartender. This was not normal, but had I ever been? Growing up without powers had made it easy to believe that I was.

I wanted to scream, but a drink sounded like the best thing in the world right now. Past midnight, *I should probably head home.* But instead, I asked, "Can you make a margarita?" I moved over to the bar area and sat down on one of the stools.

My lips twitched when the demon bartender glared back at me before muttering something under his breath and heading to the walk-in fridge. He came back with an armload of bottles and set them down on the counter.

"You know what's in it?" he asked.

I shrugged my shoulders. "Tequila," I said unhelpfully as he muttered to himself again.

Five minutes later, a drink in a non-margarita glass sat in front of me. Pink salt or possibly sugar on the rim of the glass. The color of the drink was darker than most normal ones I had before, but the first sip seemed good. I took a bigger drink and realized that it was mostly tequila. *Damn.*

"Well?" he asked, leaning against the counter.

I smiled. "It's good."

The bartender nodded before walking into the kitchen and saying to set the glass in the sink and that he would get it tomorrow.

"Thanks," I yelled at his retreating backside.

Once he was gone, I glanced down at the "drink." *Why the hell not?* I chugged the rest of the glass. Coughing, I sat the glass down on the counter.

I stepped outside the school and stopped as my vision clouded. *That's weird. Alcohol usually doesn't affect me that much.*

"Had a little too much?"

"Gran?" I couldn't believe my eyes; she looked exactly the same as the last time I saw her thirteen years ago.

"Darling," she said, her hands clasped in front of her, "I'm so sorry I couldn't stop by earlier. I should have taken you away from him. I didn't know though. Makani had kept too many secrets, even from me."

"It's okay. You're here now," I said, stepping and swaying a little as warmth seeped into my heart at hearing my mother's name.

Gran laughed, and I stopped before her, desperately wanting to hug her, but something held me back. Maybe it was the way she stood. As if she didn't want me to get too close. Tears slipped down my cheeks as a vibrant picture of her rocking me, telling me her eccentric stories of Zodians flashed before my eyes.

"Gran, were all those stories true?"

"Of course, darling. Those stories were our history. Remember them well, and they will help move you into the future." She glanced around. "My time is limited here, so let me tell you why I came."

Limited?

"Be wary of your . . ."

I jumped at the loud bang against the concrete building. I turned around to see Bob standing in the doorway, holding the glass I used.

"Can ye not follow directions?" he asked before he huffed and slammed the door again.

Geez, grouch. I turned back around, but Gran was gone. My eyes combed the school parking lot and playground, but she wasn't there. No tracks were left in the gravel either, and of course, the aether brought back Bob's signature, which happened to remind me of old *Golden Girls* reruns.

I texted Grace as I got in my car to go home, but then the world seemed to spin. *Damn margarita!* I sent another text, and a moment later, a white light appeared. I smiled at Grace.

"Did Bob make you a drink?"

She pulled me out of the car. I handed her my keys as she pushed me into the backseat. I was too tipsy to walk around the car. A few minutes later, we were in front of Dad's house.

"Give me your hand, and I'll take you to the roof."

I turned to her. "I cannot make it. No, I cannot make it." I huffed, "I can make it. Yes!"

She shook her head as she laughed. Before I blinked, we were on the roof.

"Be careful what you order from Bob."

I nodded as she disappeared, and then I climbed into the room. *One freaking drink. Who the fuck am I?* I crashed face-first onto my bed.

Nine

EMBER

By the time I opened my eyes the next morning, the sun shone bright through the curtains. *Note to self: stay away from Bob's drinks.*

I groaned. Though after a minute, I realized there was no hangover. And I didn't really miss anything. I'd already told Dad that I was skipping our morning run. I'd also magically had the day off. Two in a row was extremely rare. All was well.

A text from Grace read *None of the girls were found last night,* and it reminded me that Luke agreed to training today.

Clattering came from below. I tapped into the aether as it snaked through the house, revealing Dad was making lunch. I grabbed a pair of workout clothes from the floor, smelling them first. I threw them on before heading downstairs. I sat at the table after Dad waved me in. He set a bowl in front of me. I scooped up the first bite of ramen, savoring the warmth as I slurped in the noodles.

"Did you have a late night?" he asked after several spoonfuls.

I shrugged, not that I could tell him about the secret meeting I went to.

"Are you coming down with something?" He placed his hand upon mine. His eyes shone with concern.

"No, I've been practicing and working for a few weeks straight, and I think my body needed the sleep."

He nodded and went back to his noodles.

"What are your plans for the rest of the day?" he asked as he picked up his bowl and started to wash it, waiting for me to answer. "Isn't it nice to have a normal day?" he murmured, rubbing the bowl dry.

What is a normal day? I was supposed to head to Parker Elementary, but joining a gang doesn't sound like a normal day. "I'm heading out to the range now that I've gotten enough sleep."

He nodded. "I'll be staging a house the rest of the day. Probably be late before I get home tonight. Don't wait on me for supper."

I chirped a goodbye before heading to get ready for the day.

On my way to the range, I drove by the dollar store and decided to stop since Doug mentioned a truck would be coming with candle restocks. I parked in the back row, but before I could head in, a county cruiser screeched to a halt in front of the store. The officers jumped out, pulling their guns and running into the building. I leaned against my car, shielding my eyes from the bright sun. I watched the scene. The deputies walked out with Doug in hand-cuffs. *What the fuck?* I walked closer to hear Doug's shouts.

"I didn't do it. Someone took her! Please listen to me! She sent me a voicemail; listen to it. The monsters took her. She needs help! I'm not crazy," he yelled as the offi-cers dragged him away. He caught me in the crowd. "Em. You have to help. You have to save her."

I didn't understand what he was saying. Monsters? Did he mean Hannah? I hadn't heard from her today.

Doug continued to shout. His voice muffled after they put him into the car. Another cruiser pulled in before the officers pulled out with Doug in tow.

I needed answers. "What happened?" I asked the closest officer, who was assuring other citizens.

When he lifted his head in my direction, a slow grin appeared on his face. *Tucker.* An image of standing behind the bleachers during a football game one Friday night long ago came to mind. His arms wrapped around me before Luke shooed him away.

"Emma Ellington," he said. He came closer, standing in front of me, blocking the light from my face.

"Hey, Tucker, and yes, I'm back in town," I said, knowing he would ask. "What happened? You know Doug isn't crazy. What's going on? Is Hannah okay?"

We were in the same class back in the day. Doug may have been more computer nerd than athlete but he wasn't crazy and would never hurt Hannah.

Tucker ran his hand through his hair. I could tell he wanted to speak, but his job wouldn't allow him.

I touched his arm, stepping closer to him. "Please. Is something wrong?"

"Hannah's missing."

"Then what was that? What happened?"

Tucker turned to see the other officer talking to an elderly woman. He grabbed my arm, steering me further away from the crowd. "Apparently Doug got a voicemail from Hannah."

"And?" I prompted.

His face turned white. "Hannah's voice comes through, screaming that she's being chased by monsters before you can hear her being thrown to the ground. The message cuts off after that."

Oh god, the vampires from the other night. They had gone after Hannah, too. And succeeded. "What's the sheriff doing? Arresting Doug isn't the answer."

"He wants to keep it quiet." Tucker turned back around. Heavy sounds on the pavement penetrated our conversation. "I've got to go," he said before squeezing my arm.

I hurried back to the car. This wasn't good.

By the time I made it to the school to see Luke, the sun had dipped into early evening.

I stopped at the spot where my grandmother had been standing the night before. *Why hadn't she stuck around?* She could have answered everything I needed since Dad was so unwilling. I didn't even get a chance to write down her number. *I hope she comes back now that she knows where I am.*

"Grace said you drank one of Bob's drinks," Luke said as I walked into the cafeteria before I could tell him about Hannah missing.

"Did she tell everyone?" I asked, sitting down next to him on the same stool I used last night.

He laughed. "Of course she did."

I'll never live that down. "I didn't think one margarita would be that bad."

Luke scrunched up his nose at my preferred drink. "He makes his drinks strong, but he's not particularly fond of that one."

I glanced over at him at the way he said "that one." "Why?"

Bob grunted from the kitchen door. "It was my brother's drink, and he could make a mean one. I've never come close."

I turned to him. "Doesn't your brother have the recipe?"

Bob turned away from me and headed back into the kitchen. I glanced at Luke.

"His brother went missing several weeks ago."

"Like the girls?"

"He's not sure," Luke said, standing. "Let's go into the gym."

I followed Luke down the hall. He looked at me over his shoulder. "What?" he asked.

I shook my head and continued on, but he stopped in the middle of the hall.

"What is it?" he asked again. "Your face is all scrunched up."

"Is it weird having Bob here?"

"Why?" He turned and started walking.

I sprinted to catch up with him. "Because he's a demon," I whispered.

Luke stopped again, and I ran into his solid figure. Heat scaled my cheeks. *That hasn't changed.*

Luke leaned in, whispering back, "Yeah, and Grace is part angel. It doesn't make you a monster."

I knew that. It was what I wanted to show Dad. "But do you really know him?"

Luke shrugged. "He's never given me a reason to distrust him. There are a few others that come in every now and then. They mostly bullshit with each other, but it gives them a safe place to stay in the daylight."

We reached the gym doors, but I couldn't hold the thought any longer. "Hannah's missing. We need to find her."

Luke nodded. "Yeah, the scanner reported it about an hour ago." He shook his head. "The sheriff's an idiot arresting Doug, thinking that will keep everyone silent. There have been too many women taken."

"What are we going to do?"

He glanced down at me. "You're doing it. Let's train, and then you can help track down Hannah and the rest."

We walked into the gym that had improved since the last time I played dodgeball. Weight equipment lined one side of the room with mats laid in the center. The other side housed a cork board with wire shelves that held swords, knives, and other weapons I couldn't identify.

"Wow."

He gave me a sheepish look. "I get very bored during the day since I don't sleep much."

"I'm not judging. My friend in Berkeley has a wall of weapons, but it's not this extensive." I glanced over at Luke and continued, "She's sort of my mentor for my powers. She's helped me control them for the last few years. I think we were working up to the fighting, but she never outright said it."

He didn't waste time. "Get in position. You said your dad taught you basic self-defense in high school."

Since I could walk, but who cares about the minor details? I nodded and stepped into position. My legs shoulder width apart, facing my attacker, Luke, with my palms up in front of my face.

I made eye contact with Luke; he lunged forward, swinging at my face.

I deflected the blow, vibrating from the strength of the impact. Shaken, I closed my eyes, but being tapped into the aether, I was still aware of my surroundings. Sensing the next move, I blocked his punch.

I opened my eyes and caught the look of surprise on his face. He darted forward again, and we danced around the mat. Swinging, blocking, and circling before Luke paused once more.

"I thought your dad taught you basic self-defense."

I repositioned from the last attack. "He did."

Luke stood on the other side of the mat, drenched in sweat, his cutoff shirt clung to his muscular chest. He pulled the bottom of his shirt up to wipe his face, revealing his sleek abs. "This is way more advanced than basic self-defense techniques."

I shrugged.

Luke tossed his hair out of his eyes before coming at me again.

I didn't have time to contemplate his statement before I was keeping up with every jab. He advanced, his steps sure as I stepped back, bringing up my arms to block. My foot wobbled as I stepped on the edge of the mat. I tried to sidestep but my feet got tangled, and Luke struck one last time. Without secure footing, I couldn't take the force of the blow, and I fell back toward the hard floor. Luke grabbed my arm, twisting us to land on the mat.

I stared down at him, his hands on my hips to steady me. The tips of his ears were turning red.

He nodded once. "You're good. Come back tomorrow for a trial run." He pushed gently, and I rolled onto the mat.

Luke disappeared, leaving in a blink of an eye, the breeze ruffling my hair. I lay on the floor breathing hard. It wasn't like I was out of shape. I brought my hand to my cheek. It felt hot. It'd been four years since I'd seen him. *I'm over him.*

I climbed to my feet and reached for my phone to text Grace, wanting to see if she'd heard about Hannah. I needed to talk to Luke about how the patrols would work before I started, but he wasn't in the cafeteria. No one was. Déjà vu assaulted me when I stepped outside. The aether brought forth a feeling I knew but couldn't place. *Someone's here.*

The urgency in the aether's vibrations increased, compelling me to hide beside the building near the back play yard. Voices grew louder at the edge of the building. *Luke.* He stood beside the swing set, and a younger man stood a few feet from him.

The unwelcome stranger's hair shone in the moonlight. It seemed white, but somehow the aether told me it was blonde.

"I've seen you before," Luke said. Then he spoke louder, "Who the fuck are you? What the hell are you doing here?"

I leaned against the rough surface of the building as I listened to the refined voice of the younger man. "*We* are Gods. Why don't *you* act like it?"

"What the fuck are you talking about? Who are you?" Luke asked again.

"It doesn't matter. My plans are already unfolding. Save me the trouble and play by the rules this time," he said before disappearing.

I stared at the empty space only to bump against the wall when the young man appeared before me.

"You look familiar."

He was inches from me, and this close, I could see that his hair was platinum blonde and he had high cheekbones. His skin was smooth but pale. *Vampire?*

He leaned in closer and whispered into my ear, "It's bad business to listen where you're not wanted."

I gasped at the implication, but he was gone.

"Ember," Luke yelled. "Are you okay?"

I nodded as he pulled me out of my hidey-hole. "Who was that?"

He shook his head. "Go home." And he vanished again.

Fine, don't tell me.

Ten

EMBER

I didn't go home. My hands fidgeted around the steering wheel as I drove out to the range. With the energy drumming in my veins, I needed a good session. Lights flickered on as I stood under the covered patio. Plus, I was going to have fun picturing Luke as one of the targets. *Nobody should keep secrets—especially these men.*

I sighed. *This is all crazy, right?* Dad's choice for me to be normal was the easier option than dealing with vampires, demons, and missing women. Why was using my abilities bad? Why did Dad hate them so much? There was something I was missing. What's the point in having these powers if I couldn't help? To see Hannah's smiling face again. To hear her giggling stories. I could control fire for a reason, and that was to bring her back to Doug.

Luke mentioned once a long time ago that I was a people pleaser, except the only person I wanted to please was my dad. If I dipped my toes in the supernatural world, it wouldn't please Dad. Would he forgive me? My chest tightened as if a ticking bomb was about to explode. I didn't know for sure. I knew he loved me. It had all seemed so much easier on paper when I listed out my goals for coming home in June.

I shook away the thoughts as I gazed at the edge of the range where the one lamp still worked. I wouldn't be able to see if I hit the bullseye from this distance, but that wouldn't stop me.

I stepped off the concrete when a flash of white light blinded me. My hand tightened around the grip of the bow as I reached for an arrow in my limited vision. I turned to the right, ready to shoot whatever popped in unexpectedly.

"Damnit, Grace. Is it your goal in life to scare me half to death?"

I turned back to the target and released the arrow. It soared through the air. Again, thanks to the broken overhead light, I could only hear the echo in the darkness.

"Of course. What are you doing? I can't believe Hannah was taken." She kicked one of the melted candles I missed cleaning yesterday.

"We will find Hannah." I laid my bow on the concrete table.

She sat down, pulling at my jacket. "Talk to me. Does this mean you're going to help the others?"

"Yes," I said without hesitation. I bit my lip and sat down beside Grace. "Luke thinks I know enough about fighting, but I'm worried. Using my powers doesn't come naturally to me. What if I fail and someone gets hurt because of me?" Grace reached around me, trying to pull me in, but I shook my head. "When those vampires tried to take me, I would have been a goner if Luke hadn't showed. I managed to block some of their attacks, but they were superfast, and I couldn't stay toe to toe with them."

"You don't mean that." She squeezed me tight. "You'll get better. It takes practice, and besides, that was the first time."

"What if I don't?" I said and turned to watch the one good lamp flicker in the darkness. "What if I'm better off without these powers?"

"Why would you think that?"

"The bind lifted two years ago. The fire controls me more than I control it. It's still a struggle each day to keep it in check."

"You got this. Look how long it took you to get archery." She giggled beside me. "Remember when you told me your dad wouldn't let you eat breakfast until you hit the target? And after I told my dad, he always packed an extra sausage muffin for me to give you when we met at school?"

My smile didn't reach the wideness of Grace's, since I knew that was true. Ten-year-old Grace hadn't realized that I truly had to earn my breakfast. Those first few years of archery were tough, but like she said, I managed and got through them.

I nodded. "You're right. I'm a National Champion. It will take some time to learn my flames."

"That gives me an idea."

I glanced at her. Her ideas weren't usually the best but always fun, like the one time we hauled her mattress to the top of the stairs and surfed until her parents came home.

"What if you bring your bow out with you? It will give you more security if your powers don't work the way you think they will."

Use what I'm good at to supplement my powers? I embraced Grace, and she squeaked. "That's perfect. I'll have a backup."

Grace stood. "I knew you would love it when it came to me. Anyway, I will see you tomorrow at the school."

"Okay," I said as Grace disappeared in a ball of light again.

I checked the time. Morning would come too soon, but I wanted to complete the long-range targets before I called it. *Did I have enough time to practice making fireballs?*

The darkness swept in around me as I debated. If someone drove on the road beside the range, they might see light from my fire and investigate. What would I tell them? I sighed, worried for nothing. Dad and I were the only ones who came out here, and he was working late tonight.

I fired off the remaining arrows in the quiver. I switched my bow from the left to the right as I headed to grab the arrows.

I plucked the arrows from the bullseye under the broken lamp. With the last arrow retrieved, I headed back to the patio to put the rest of my gear away.

The aether stirred, bringing death and decay, and I knew I wasn't alone anymore. The similarities from the other night filtered in. *Vampires.*

Two figures walked out of the tall prairie grass on the edge of the property line as I notched an arrow. I held my breath as they got closer. They, like Grace, disappeared but instead grew closer.

Arrow ready, I glanced at the sneer on the guy's face.

His fangs were already covered in blood. "Not so fast, girlie. We heard you gave Titan the slip a few days ago."

I cocked my head to the side, and my hair slid away to expose the flesh of my neck. The vampire launched, but the aether helped guide my arrow. It struck dead center. I nailed the heart. *Piece of cake.*

The vampire stopped, looked at the arrow, and his smile widened. "Like this arrow could kill me," he mocked.

I paused. *Wouldn't it?* And then it hit me: the arrow was made of aluminum. I needed wood. A stake like the one Luke carried. *Shit.*

The aether stirred, and I turned to meet the second vampire too late. He gripped my neck, lifting me off the ground. My feet dangled as he wrenched the bow from my grasp. It clamored to the ground.

I tried to bring in air as I brought my hands up to loosen his grip. When that didn't work, I struck out against his face. He swayed, and his grip loosened, but he didn't let go. I took in oxygen.

I tried to pry the icy fingers from my skin once more.

He countered, tightening his grip. I wheezed, but I couldn't wedge the vampire's hand free.

Calm.

I tried to take a deep inhale to center myself, but my breath caught.

"Don't kill her," his companion yelled from behind me.

Why did they want me alive? Why were they kidnapping women?

I tried to concentrate on bringing forth my fire. I grabbed the vampire's wrist as flame sparked from my fingertips. It flickered as the vampire's eyes widened. He squeezed tighter, and the sparks faded.

No.

I struggled for air; the sparks moved closer to me, and like magic, they roared to life. The flame caught, and his hand was no longer attached to his body.

I dropped to the ground.

He opened his mouth to speak, but nothing came out as the flames spread from his wrist through the rest of his body.

I stood, ripped off the vampire's burning hand, and tossed it to the ground beside the rest of the ashes.

I turned to the remaining monster. "So, let's talk." I took small, measured steps toward him. He made no attempt to move as he watched me, the arrow still stuck in his heart. His face was similar to the vampire from the other day except less intense.

He didn't seem worried as he gripped the arrow and pulled. "Don't get cocky. I'll bring you in for that rewa . . ." His words disappeared with him. As soon as he pulled the arrow out, his body turned gray.

I watched as another pile of ash joined the first one. "What the fuck?"

I bent to retrieve the arrow where the vampire discarded it on the ground. I scanned the arrow under the working light. It was made of aluminum, but the arrowhead was a different material. I had always assumed metal, but maybe it was wood. Dad purchased crates of these at a time. He stored them in the garage under lock and key.

I stared down at the ash and wished I'd asked my question before he pulled out the arrow. Though, in my defense, I didn't know that would happen.

Now if the smell of decay would disappear, and just like that, the wind whistled through the grass carrying the ashes away.

Eleven

EMBER

I stood in front of the demon barkeep.

"You want another drink?"

I shook my head. "No, I learned my lesson. What did you put in it? I don't usually get tipsy."

Bob cocked his head to the side and smiled. "That's because you're used to drinking the watered-down versions for humans. I make my drinks for the customer. Since you're Zodian, I knew you could take more than normal." He scratched his horn. "But you're only half."

My first sip of alcohol had come during the second year of college, when Vanessa had finally talked me into going to a bar her cousin was able to sneak us into. It took three drinks before Vanessa started spouting love to random strangers. After five drinks, Evie cut me off even though nothing seemed different. Evie just laughed and said I would start to feel the effects soon. The next day I nursed Vanessa through her hangover and marveled at not being sick. And each and every time after that, I would be fine except for the night of my birthday.

"If you didn't come for a drink. What do you want?" the surly demon asked.

I turned my head back to the cafeteria. "Where are the others?" I wasn't late, but no one else was here either.

The demon leaned back, placing his hands on his belly before he started laughing. He was still chuckling as he walked into the kitchen without answering.

Ass. "Hey," I yelled, but either he didn't hear or didn't care. I walked back over to a table to wait, scrolling through social media.

A light flashed throughout the dimmed room. "Awe." I shielded my eyes.

Grace sat down on the other side. "So, I have bad news," she started.

I lowered my hand. "Let's not talk about bad news."

"I know I said I could go out with you on your first night, but the Collective needs me to do something else."

"Tell them you'll do it later," I whined.

"I can't. They're the bosses," she said.

"Who are *they* exactly?" I asked.

She looked down at her watch. "I don't have time to explain. Ask me later." She vanished from the room.

Five minutes later. I glanced down at my watch. *Where was everyone?* Bored, I stood and headed down the hallway, relieved I remembered the layout of the school. The cafeteria was in the basement with a few of the older classrooms and janitor closets. Most of the classrooms were on the top floor. The ground level held the offices, nurse's office, and gym.

I walked down the hallway lit by emergency lights. Nothing really to see as the classrooms were shut. Deadbolted from the outside. This area was clean like the cafeteria. I turned left down the hallway toward the janitor closet, hearing voices through the slightly open door.

"I don't understand." Kaity's voice filtered down the hallway. "We're meant to be together."

"I'm sorry." It was Luke's voice.

He paused, and I knew he probably heard me.

I retreated back down the hallway. Once in the lunchroom, I sighed. *I'm glad I didn't walk into that awkwardness.* Ted and Nathan had arrived and were chatting at a table. I joined them to wait for Kaity and Luke.

"Hey guys," I said after getting settled.

Ted glanced away at my greeting, but Nathan pointed his finger in my face.

"You can't just walk back into Luke's life like nothing happened." He huffed. "He was really broken because of you."

I opened my mouth to speak, but Ted cut in.

"You agreed to marry him and then left without a trace. I didn't think you were like that, but now I'll be watching you."

"*We* will be watching you." Nathan made a *v* sign with his fingers and brought them to his eyes and flung them back my way.

Honestly, I didn't blame them, but it wasn't them I

needed to apologize to. It was Luke, and he deserved to know everything from me. Lately, though, it never seemed like the right time or place.

Kaity appeared first; her jaw clenched as she sat down beside me.

Luke appeared a moment after her. He started the meeting, which included news that none of the women had been found. He split us into two teams and assigned areas. Ted's eyes shot daggers as he left with Nathan.

Sighing, I stood to head outside when Kaity grasped my hand and Luke's shirt, transporting us in a blink of an eye to what Dad called a "realtor nightmare." This area was known for its drug dens. The police monitored it more than any other sections of town.

"Keep close," Luke said as he started off.

I kept pace with Kaity as we walked behind him. I looked over, and her body was tense as she literally stomped beside me. Her face was frozen in a disapproving look as she eyed the back of Luke's head.

"You okay?" I asked as our pace slowed farther behind Luke.

She glanced over at me. "I'm fine. Just wishing I could set someone on fire." She eyed Luke again.

"I could help," I said, trying to lighten her mood. "Fire is my department."

She stopped, completely taken aback with my answer. And she smiled. "I'll let you know."

Her mood seemed better as she stopped pounding her feet into the pavement, and we set a better pace.

Hours later, I trudged through the mud, one step

behind Luke as his eyes searched the distance. This part of town consisted of tiny houses sandwiched together, barely room to walk between them. Some architect's idea of copying shotgun houses in Louisiana.

I reached to grab the straps of the quiver, tightening them once more. I'd yet to pull an arrow from its sleeve, but after the vampire's attack at the range, I would be ready. *Mostly.*

My mind wandered between the task at hand and Doug's arrest. The cold vampire's fingers on my throat, and the disappointed look on Luke's face that first night. Dad's whisper floated through my mind. *A normal life is what you want.*

I made my own voice stronger. *This could be normal too.* I surveyed the land again; vampires in this town needed to be stopped. Grace had been extremely pleased that I'd defeated two vampires by myself before officially going on patrol tonight. After I sent my message off to her last night, she sent back a range of emojis.

So far, we had been at this for three hours, and there'd been nothing. I listened as the aether stirred around me, bringing with it the first sign of trouble. Someone watched from between the houses, but I couldn't tell which house as they were so close together. Luke's body tensed up ahead, and I was thankful that I didn't need to tell him. I didn't really know how to explain the aether to anyone.

He paused in the road. Kaity and I came to his side. I searched the road, the houses, and in between but spotted nothing.

"Did you hear anything?" Luke asked beside me.

"No, we don't have your hearing," Kaity said, stepping away from the group and heading back in the direction we came. "You hear things from miles away. Are you sure there's something here?"

Luke huffed beside me. "Are you doubting my hearing?"

Kaity whipped around. "Are you serious? No, I'm not doubting your hearing, old man, but maybe for once, it's not what you think it is."

"And maybe, like always, I'm right about this too."

"You know, being out here in the road could cause suspicion," I said in an attempt to deflate the tension.

While it was early morning, someone could be awake for work watching three young people walk the street. While Luke hid his knives in his coat and Kaity carried nothing but her magic, I stuck out like a sore thumb. A bow in my hand with arrows sticking over my back.

Luke broke eye contact with Kaity. "It's getting close to sunrise. We should head back to the school before that happens."

I nodded, and as a group, we pivoted to start our trek back to the school. I reached my hand out in Kaity's direction, but she kept walking. *Guess we're really walking back.* I glanced at my muddy shoes. *I need to buy a cheaper pair.*

Luke jumped in front of me, pushing against my shoulder.

Startled, I lost my balance and landed in the mud.

My bow landed a few inches away from me. One end of it stuck into the mud.

I wiped the mud from my hands. Vampires sprinted toward us, but Luke was already in a shuffle with one. Kaity was throwing fireballs on the other side of me.

I grabbed my bow and gave it a quick thrust hoping the mud would be dislodged. In a crouch, I looked around. Seven vampires surrounded us. Four were swarming Luke and Kaity while the other three held back around the perimeter.

Perfect. I notched the first arrow and took aim. The surprise on the vampire's face was priceless until the mud that had been stuck on the bowstring flung back into my face. I swiped at the mud, but I wasn't fast enough. The other vampires were aware of me now. I notched another arrow, but mud ran down my face. I released the arrow before sighting the vampire's heart. Lifting my arm, I attempted to wipe away the dirt.

The arrow skimmed the monster's arm. *Shit.* The aether was overloaded with all the vampire signatures. Most of them smelled of dust and decay, but some smelled of blood and dirt. I took a breath and threads appeared in my vision. It flickered and vanished. I grabbed another arrow from my quiver and took a deeper breath. A thread appeared again attached to the vampire I missed. I notched the third arrow and let it fly. *Bullseye.*

The two vampires I'd hit smiled, and flashes of last night popped into my mind. Together, they pulled the arrows out and discarded them on the ground. Their bodies began to disintegrate.

"Behind you," Luke yelled.

I turned to meet the cold eyes of the last three. I didn't have time for an arrow. I swung my bow, catching the monster off guard. He stepped back into Luke's waiting stake.

I looked around at the seven piles of ash before the wind carried them down the street.

"Good work," Luke said beside me. "You need to keep a focus on the moving pieces though."

Kaity scoffed beside me. "You need a bath."

I looked down at my clothes. Mud caked my entire left side where Luke had pushed me. I brushed back a piece of hair only to find more dirt there. I glanced to see Kaity scrunch her nose as she started back toward Parker Elementary. Luke only paused a moment; he had a half grin on his face before he, too, fell in step behind Kaity.

"Ugh." I followed behind them at a much slower rate.

I didn't even bother to go into the school when we arrived. I made it home in no time but should've found something to lay on the seat. Now mud caked that too.

Not wanting to get mud on the floors in the house, I walked around the yard. When I got to the back, I reached to pull myself onto the window sill. A groan later, I rolled onto the roof, but as I opened the window, I realized I needed to discard the muddy clothes. Pushing the aether out to make sure the neighbors on either side were asleep, I sighed when all was quiet. I hurriedly took off my shoes, pants, and shirt before climbing into my room. After grabbing pj's, I walked to the bathroom.

"Em, you're awake. Great. I'll meet you in ten minutes," Dad's voice said below.

I raised my hands to hide the dirt in my hair but realized with no lights on that Dad couldn't see me.

"Sure," I uttered back as I shut the bathroom door. "Crap."

Twelve

EMBER

"Why did you come home?"

I glanced at the man beside me. *Vampire,* or that's what the others said. I couldn't figure out why his aether was different from the others I had come across over the past few days. Could it be because I'd known him before he was a vampire?

"I came home to find answers."

"Answers?" Luke asked as we started down an alley that would cut into the Shiner's Park.

I kept pace with him as we walked while I mulled over what to share. "I know nothing about my mother."

"You mentioned before that she died when you were young."

I flexed my arm holding the bow and wished I'd remembered the strap tonight. Pavement met grass at the park entrance. It was overgrown with weeds, litter in piles, and the surrounding fence leaned heavily to one side. *It had once been a nice place to take in nature.*

We stepped through the rusted gate, heading directly through to the center of the park. No one hung out here anymore. Vampires brought victims here to drain their blood, so Luke insisted whoever covered this area of town swung through the forgotten park.

"My grandmother once told me that The Cross killed my mother, but I can't get Dad to tell me anymore or confirm what Gran said."

Luke stopped and turned toward me with a smile on his face. "The Cross, as in staked to one?"

"I don't know, I know it sounds ridiculous. I was five when she told me, and I put it out of my mind. But she told me stories of vampires and werewolves too." I shrugged my shoulders. "And those are true. Why couldn't that be true? I need to figure out what The Cross means."

"The Cross seems pretty vague?"

I shook my head again. "Which is why I came back to get answers from my dad."

Luke opened his mouth to speak but disappeared before my eyes. *Stupid vampire speed.* With the aether, I searched, eyes closed. Movement to my left brought my bow arm level. I opened my eyes again. Aimed. Fired. Thud.

I stepped closer to see that my arrow missed the vampire but pierced his leather jacket to strike the tree behind. Pinned for a second. He struggled to pull the arrow out of the wood when Luke reappeared and forced him to the tree again.

"Who are you?" Luke shoved the vampire, lifting him from the ground.

I notched another arrow as I came to stand beside Luke.

"Who are you?" he asked again.

The vampire snarled at Luke, but when his eyes caught sight of me, they widened.

"Do you know her?" Luke asked, noticing the cue.

The vampire struggled, but Luke wasn't letting him go. The vampire stopped; his eyes, dead of any life, glared at Luke.

"Did you think you could have a snack and go on your way?"

"No," the vampire muttered.

"No?" I asked, "Why were you in the park? And better yet, why are you in this town?"

We waited as the vampire weighed his options. Luke had his stake positioned over the guy's heart. If the vampire moved a little, he would be no more.

"I'm looking for a friend?"

"Friend or vampire?"

I lowered my bow, leaving the arrow notched as I waited for an answer.

"Friend, but a vampire. Rumor has him in this town."

"What for?"

The vampire turned his head away from us.

"What's your name?" I asked from behind Luke.

He turned to look at me, his eyes widening again. "You look like—" He stopped. "Cliff."

I didn't know what he was going to say about my looks, but I continued, "Cliff, nice to meet you. I'm Ember, and we need to know what your friend is doing here in town. We could help each other." Luke gave me a look, but I ignored him. Cliff seemed to differ from the other vampires I met. "How old are you?" He still smelled like death and decay, but it was muted compared to the others.

Cliff looked back at me. "Five hundred."

"That's why you seem in control of the blood lust?"

He nodded.

Luke edged the stake closer. "Why is your friend in town?"

"He tangled himself with the Chaos Brothers."

"Chaos Brothers," I whispered. *Why did that sound familiar?*

"And what do the Chaos Brothers want with the residents of Happy Valley?" Luke said.

Cliff glanced back at me. "He's searching for the Zodian Warrior."

"The women?" Luke whispered. "The vampires have been kidnapping women because they think one of them is the Zodian Warrior?"

Cliff didn't answer, but his eyes darted behind us. I turned, but Luke caught me mid-turn. He wrapped his arms around my shoulders, pushing me to the ground. The loud thud overshadowed my gasp.

I coughed as Luke rolled off. He disappeared again as I looked to Cliff, but he was no longer there. A pile of ash lay at the bottom of the tree. I climbed to my feet, retrieved my bow, and connected with the aether. Nothing but Luke was in the vicinity.

A broken piece of fence stuck out from the tree beside my arrow. I stepped to get a closer look at the post. I pulled the arrow free and replaced it in the quiver as Luke reappeared.

"Anything?"

He shook his head. "No, I heard the whistle."

"Fence," I muttered and pointed to the splintered post.

Luke pulled it out of the tree. "The killer listened in on our conversation."

"Which means what? He didn't want Cliff to tell us anything else? What else could there be? We now know that the Chaos Brothers, whoever they are, are after the Zodian Warrior, and we don't know who either of them are. We know that none of the women taken from Happy Valley could be the Zodian Warrior," I chirped, counting the incidents on my hand.

"Except you."

I turned to look at Luke. *Except me.* He had a point. Could I be the Zodian Warrior? *Could that be the reason my mother was killed?*

Thirteen

EMBER

I placed the padlock to the garage on top of the deep freezer before flipping the light on. The tiny space held several boxes of my dad's "for sale" signs. I spied my prize at the back. I opened the crate stamped with Anita's Curiosities to find more arrows. Dad ordered them from a shop in Berkeley and always had a surplus. I gathered some to take back with me. The three left in my quiver would be happy to have friends.

"What are you doing?" Dad stood in the doorway.

"I needed more. Knew I could count on you to have these."

He looked at the arrows. "Of course, Emma."

"Ember," I muttered, turning away from him.

"Em. Yes, I keep them stocked."

"These are way better than the arrows the Berkeley team used."

He smiled. "Better quality. Make sure you aren't losing too many."

He grabbed the padlock from the freezer and placed it back on the garage door as we headed out.

"Do you want me to cook one of your favorites tonight?" he asked.

I shook my head. He knew I planned to go out with Grace. *Why did he even ask?* We walked in silence through the house.

"Do you want to go for a run? It's hotter than normal, but I could use the exercise," I said, laying the arrows on the kitchen table.

He glanced out at the dwindling sky and nodded.

We met back outside after changing. Our pace began slowly at the beginning but picked up. The late afternoon heat wasn't as bad as I thought it would be for this time of year.

We stopped at our midway point. I jogged in place as Dad took a sip of water.

"Let's walk back."

I turned to look at the strictest person I'd ever known. "You want to walk back?" *Did he have a fever?* I looked at him but didn't see any signs of sickness. "All right."

"Can we talk?" he asked and continued before I answered. "How is the bank working out?"

"Oh." I stepped beside him as we marched back to the house. "It's okay."

"Not exactly what you went to school for, I know, but it's at least making some money."

"It's honestly not that bad. Um, now that you mention it. I have a job waiting for me back in Berkeley."

He turned to look at me. "Berkeley?"

"Yeah, my friend, Evie, works for a big corporation and said she could hire me in their communication department."

Dad stopped in the middle of the street. "Why did you come home then?"

I turned to look him in the face. Maybe this wasn't the best time, but we'd already headed down this road. "The main reason is to know more about my mother."

"You came back because of your mother," he repeated. "We could have talked about her on the phone. I don't understand why you would pass up a job offer. One that could give you a normal life."

Was he joking? His jaw tensed, waiting for me to respond.

I clenched my fists. "When would you have talked to me about her on the phone?" I said slowly, "Every time I mentioned her or asked you a question, you deflected it to something else. So yes, Dad, I came home in the hopes of getting answers face-to-face. She was my mother, and I only know her name. She was a Zodian, but you won't tell me what the hell that means."

"Quiet," he hissed, looking up and down the deserted road.

"There's no one around." I waved my arms. "I need to know her. I want to know how she died."

"You don't need to hear that."

"But you've never told me. You never talk about her. She was part of both of our lives. How can you just cut her out? She was your wife and my mother."

"Em, it doesn't matter now. It's in the past, and you

should look forward to your future," he said and glanced back toward the house. "You should focus on that new job in Berkeley. A normal job and a normal life. I know what is best for you. And, well, I've been thinking of returning to Berkeley myself. I can be closer to my aging parents and you."

He smiled back at me as he started toward the house. "Wouldn't it be nice to be closer together? I've only been staying here for you."

I gritted my teeth as I caught back up to him. "Do you know anything about Zodian Warriors?"

He paused mid-step. "Where did you hear that?" His voice came out harsh as his eyes pierced me.

Shit. How did I explain I knew about it without telling him I was hunting vampires at night with my friends?

"Um," I stuttered.

"Emma."

He grabbed my elbow, and I instantly pulled away from him.

"Emma?" He questioned my reaction.

"Ember," I hissed. "I searched the internet for Zodian last night, and it's a possible match."

His breathing slowed as he stared at me. I couldn't tell if he bought my story or not. He swayed on his feet as he broke eye contact before starting toward home.

"Dad!" I sprinted to catch his fast walk.

He stopped again, turning to me. "You do not need to know about any of that."

"But," I started, and he hushed me.

"I'm done talking about this," he yelled loud enough for anyone in the vicinity to hear. "Just listen to me. I don't want to hear another question about your mother."

He left me in the middle of the road as I reeled over his anger. He wouldn't answer any questions. *Why?*

He dismissed me yet again. I clenched my fists as I jogged past him without a word. At this rate, I would end up burning something down. I needed to get away and clear my head. *How can it not be important?* My mother. She was part of my DNA.

"Agh!" I didn't stay long at the house before I threw my gear in the trunk of my car and headed out to the range. The way I burned inside, I would be out there until it was time for us to patrol.

⇥

I avoided Dad the rest of the day but couldn't ignore Ted now as we walked side by side. Despite the fact that he was only human, he went out almost as much as everyone else and managed to do fairly well in fights considering he spent most of his time on his computer.

"Stop pouting," he muttered beside me as we came through the same park where Luke and I'd met Cliff.

"I'm not pouting," I issued back as I scanned the landscape before me. I doubted any new vampires would show their faces here with Luke's signature written all over the place.

He huffed. "You forget that I've known you for a while. You're pouting. Probably something about your dad, even though you never mention your home life. The little I know comes from Grace's big mouth."

"Geez, I'm not pouting."

He huffed again but didn't say anything else as we made our last round in the park. I was ready for bed and hoped the anger toward Dad had dissipated. I didn't want to hate him.

I stopped as an image of death and decay swarmed the aether. Bringing my bow forward, I snatched an arrow from the quiver and fired at the incoming vampires. The aether guided my arrow straight through their hearts.

Ted stood at my back as we each took a side. He wielded a wood stake.

As dust drifted to the ground, the remaining vampires realized they were not winning. Several dropped back.

"They're retreating! Let's go!" Ted yelled.

I glanced over to see him sprint after a group of vampires before turning back around to slay the last one on my side. Before the dust settled, I sprinted after Ted.

I came around to the front of the park, beside the tree where Cliff had been killed, eyeing the monsters. Somehow they'd managed to capture Ted. He stood stoic as the vampire held him to his chest, his fangs out and blood dripping as it trickled down Ted's shoulder.

The vampire hissed, "You're going to let us go or I'll rip your friend's throat out."

I gripped my bow and realized the vampire had Ted

situated where I couldn't make the shot without hitting Ted.

The vampire laughed as he started to back toward the broken front gate. Ted's eyes widened, and he struggled in the vampire's hold.

If Ted disappeared right now, I knew I might never see him again.

"Torch them in flames, dear," came a soft whisper beside me.

I half turned to see Gran standing beside me. My eyes widened, but she nodded. *Trust your instincts. The flames will only burn what you want.*

"Ember," Ted yelled.

The vampire stepped back again. He had a glint in his eyes that said he was about to do that wickedly fast-paced run creepy vampires could do.

I lowered my bow slowly. "We can make a deal."

Torch them. Another whisper caught in the wind. The other vampires started forward.

"Ember."

I dropped the carbon fiber bow, holding my hands down, connecting to the aether. I directed the blaze through the ground. The energy built, and heat spread through me. The fire raced through the ground just beneath the vampire and Ted. I lifted my palms toward the sky, and the flames erupted from the earth, wrapping around them both.

More flames erupted, catching the other vampires before they could flee. Ted managed to break free from the vampire still engulfed in flames. Ted dropped onto the grass and rolled around.

I watched the last remaining ashes of the vampires fade away before releasing my energy.

I glanced over at Ted, still rolling on the ground. "Dude, you good?"

He stopped short, sat up, and looked at his body. "What?" he sputtered. "How?" He tried again.

I reached my hand out to help him stand.

We made it back to the school cafeteria where Luke sat on a barstool drinking an amber liquid. No one else was in the room.

Ted turned sharply and pointed. "She set me on fire," he yelled, finally over the shock.

I smiled, but before I could speak, Ted screamed again. He waved his arms and completed a circle.

"You're okay though. You didn't die," I stated to get him to shut up. He was acting like a loon.

Luke, by this point, had turned in our direction, watching as Ted hollered.

"Ted," I screamed to get his attention. "You're fine."

He threw his hands in the air and stomped out.

I sighed and headed over to where Luke sat.

He raised an eyebrow and asked, "You set him on fire?"

"Oh, you heard that. Geez, he's such a baby," I said, taking the bottle on the counter and pouring a glass of whatever it was. I gulped it down and coughed. "Yes, I set him on fire."

"He probably deserved it, but tell me what happened anyway."

I heard the smirk in his voice as I eyed the bottle. Before I could pour another drink, Luke had done it for me. I thanked him and took a swallow much slower than the first, then dished the details of the last hour of our patrol.

Luke smiled after I finished the story. "He'll come around. How did you know it would work?"

"I . . ." The image of Gran flooded my mind. "My Gran appeared out of nowhere. It's the second time I've seen her, but she never sticks around to talk to me. It's really weird."

Those moments with Gran were surreal. I wondered if it had to do with the aether? Was it connecting us somehow? Could Zodians even do that? Why did she never stay? All my questions could be answered.

Was there no hope of ever learning about Mom? I downed the rest of my drink.

"You better slow down," Luke said as I grabbed the bottle again.

I poured another, and he kept silent. We sat into the wee hours of the morning, drinking in silence.

Fourteen

EMBER

I tried to focus on the screen in front of me as I yawned. My job today included checking the work from yesterday's tellers. Adding and subtracting with little sleep wasn't easy. I managed a solid two hours of sleep the night before and almost regretted drinking with Luke.

The aether fizzled around me.

"Hey." Kaity leaned against the teller counter.

I shifted my feet. "Hey, what can I help you with?" I asked.

"When do you get off?"

I glanced at the computer screen to get the time. Four hours had passed by so quickly. "In fifteen minutes actually."

Kaity straightened, a smile on her face. "Awesome. Do you wanna grab lunch?"

I tried to hide my sigh, but her lips wavered. "I

packed lunch today because I wanted to go out to the range."

"Range?"

"Yeah. You know the gun range out on the outskirts of town?"

"People use that?"

I laughed. "It's just me most days."

"Can I go with you?" she asked.

"Um." I didn't need to hide my abilities since she knew about them. "Yeah. Why don't you grab some lunch, and we can eat out there."

She nodded and turned but halfway through the lobby, threw over her shoulder, "I'll meet you out front in twenty minutes." At that, some of the other customers looked over at me.

I smiled at them as Kaity sailed out the revolving door.

Denise headed my direction, a frown on her face. "You're hanging out with her?"

I nodded. Her frown didn't disappear. "What do you know about her?"

Denise turned her back to the customers before answering in a whisper, "She lives across the street from me. Her dad walked out on her and her mom several years ago. Never came back. Her mom died a few months ago due to cancer. Sad thing is she doesn't have any other family to take her in. What's even stranger is that I know the power to her house turned off last week, but I've seen lights on at night, and it's not candlelight."

I never knew my mother. Kaity, having known her

mother and losing her to such a miserable disease, must have been tough. And now she went out at night to kill the vampires that lurked in this town.

I locked eyes with Denise, her taking my blank stare as an opening to continue gossiping about how Kaity was unfit to maintain that big house of hers. *How awful to lose your mom and then have to choose whether to keep the lights on or food on the table.*

Memories of my childhood floated to the surface of times before we came to Happy Valley. Dad would leave me with an elderly neighbor, reminding me to be good in a stern voice. The lady laughed, saying I was one of the most well-behaved kids she'd ever watched, not knowing the small lecture went beyond being good. He'd meant no fire. I promised myself I would be normal every morning.

The small rental house we lived in barely had room for one adult man, let alone a kid who had uncontrollable fits and set furniture on fire. Now looking back, I knew why we left in the middle of the night.

"Did the power to her house get turned off because she couldn't get access to the insurance money from her mother's death?" I asked.

"I've never believed there was any insurance money. It wasn't like the mother ever worked a day in her life . . ."

I didn't understand why Denise was this way, but I knew it would take a lot to change her mind.

". . . There were always weird sounds coming from that house even before her mother died."

That same resistance in Denise's body was what Dad had in his when I asked questions about my mother.

Why were they like this? I shook my head. "Thanks, Denise, but I think Kaity needs a friend now more than ever."

Denise left me with a warning to be careful of the friends I chose. She, of course, didn't know that I was friends with a Nephilim and others of that nature. If Denise knew of the things that went bump in the night, which Kaity spent her time vanquishing before they could hurt the people of this town, she might think differently. *Or still be a bitch.*

My shift ended, and I headed out front to wait for Kaity, but I didn't wait long. She rushed up with a bag, the Eats! logo on the side.

"I'm ready," she yelled, the bag held above her head in her excitement.

I motioned her to the back of the bank where my old beater sat. We climbed in, and I drove us out to the range. Neither one of us talked as the outside world changed.

"Did you ever get access to your money?" I asked, turning onto the highway.

"Not yet." Kaity gripped the seatbelt. "I can't find my dad's death certificate at the house. And the city didn't have any records of it either."

"So what will you do?"

Her grip lessened as I turned down the gravel road to the range. "I'm not really sure what county he died in, just that my mom told me he was dead. I have vague memories of him as a child." She undid her seatbelt, and we exited the car. "I'll probably end up forging the documents."

I opened the trunk. "You can do that?"

She nodded. "Yeah. Mom showed me how when she got really sick and the hospital was asking for all these forms. The magic doesn't last forever but long enough to get me access to the money."

I grabbed my equipment and headed to the covered area to lay it out. "You'd better be careful. I know the money's yours, but it wouldn't be good to be investigated for fraud."

She smiled. "Don't worry. I know how to handle everything. Once the ink is done brewing, I'll have my money."

She seemed to have everything in order so I grabbed my lunch. I took a bite out of the peanut butter and jelly sandwich. Kaity purchased some type of croissant for lunch.

"Why did you want to have lunch?" I asked. Kaity didn't immediately answer so I glanced over to her. I could tell she had a mouth full. I laughed. "Sorry."

I unzipped my bag. My bow ready, I stepped to the imaginary line and took a deep breath. On my exhale, the arrow soared.

"Wow. How far is that?" Kaity asked from behind me.

"It's forty yards." I took another arrow and aimed it at the closer target. Bullseye. I turned to Kaity. "Why did you want to meet?"

She shrugged her shoulders. "I wanted to get to know you. Grace doesn't like to hang out with me." She paused, and I shot another arrow. "She doesn't like that I'm younger. And she never liked that I dated Luke."

My formation faltered at the last words, and the arrow missed the target. Dang. I glanced at Kaity to see if she noticed anything amiss. *Did she know I'd overheard their conversation?* Grace should have told me anyway. I laid my bow down and came back to my lunch.

"That doesn't seem like Grace. She's always been friendly with everyone." I laughed. "She once made friends with a slimy green frog when we were little. Her mother raged for days when she found it in her kitchen."

Kaity smiled. "I don't know. I honestly can't believe that Luke and Grace are cousins. They're like night and day. They don't really look similar either. Grace is so blonde, and Luke's so dark." She paused. "I've tried hanging out with her but she's just . . ."

I caught her looking down at the worn T-shirt that had seen better days, and I knew she felt inferior to Grace. I understood that. Being poor had caused me to question whether or not we could be friends at the beginning of our relationship. The first time I visited Grace's house, surrounded by woodlands, outside of town, I'd asked Dad if they lived in a bed and breakfast. We had stayed in one during our move to Happy Valley. It had a similar wraparound porch but was painted in a cheerful yellow with black shutters. The lawn was immaculate as we drove the long winding gravel road. His smile hadn't reached his eyes as he told me no.

"Ted says that she's changed since she got her powers, but I didn't know her before that. Luke and I dated off and on for a couple of years, but I was younger, so Grace and I never made a connection. Luke and I split permanently not long before the accident that took his parents."

"I know how you feel." I leaned against the bench where my sandwich lay. "I met Grace when I was eight and didn't realize the difference between us. As we grew, I saw the difference in the clothes we wore."

How many times had Grace's mom talked Dad into allowing me to go with them on their monthly shopping trip? Dad gave me a small amount of money to buy one shirt or one treat but nothing too extravagant since most of my clothes came from yard sales where he haggled over the price.

"Dad single-handedly raised me with one income. He got his realtor license when I was ten to support us."

He'd worked for his mother until we moved to Happy Valley when I was eight—*the year he'd given me the elixir.* I didn't remember much of what he did during those earlier years as he left me with a woman next door. When we moved here, he started working as an assistant to a local realtor until he passed the exam and became one himself. It took him several years to build the business, but now he rented an office in the commercial district of town.

Kaity stood and threw her trash in one of the various bins around the complex. "I get that. While I live in a big house, it needs a lot of work. Luke's house was impressive."

I nodded my agreement. I had at one time been awed by his parents' house. Marble countertops in the four bathrooms with real wood floors in the five bedrooms despite there being only three of them. Luke's mom, Helen, always wore an apron while baking or cleaning, similar to Grace's mom, her sister.

While the two-story house and money were great, Luke's parents had been even better. His parents were actively interested in his boxing accomplishments—always bringing a batch of freshly baked cookies to every match. They genuinely cared. They played board games after dinner. *Who does that?* The love between them lit up every room.

I stood and stretched, ready to get back to training. I looked over my shoulder at Kaity. "What type of witch are you?"

She smiled. "There are several kinds. But I'm an ancestral witch."

"Which means your powers come from your ancestors and the town they lived in." I saw that on a TV drama once a few years ago.

She moved around the benches, eyeing the area. It was broken into two main sections: the covered pavilion where concrete benches and tables sat for use, and the target area. The target area was split in four with white chalk lining the mixed grass and sand that went back three hundred yards. There were four different targets, each with different sizes at varying yards. "Yeah, pretty much."

"I wasn't aware there was a coven of witches in Happy Valley." I dug into my bag to get out the three candles. I set them on the pavement beside where I was shooting.

"There isn't. My mother's coven is back in Maine," Kaity said from behind me.

I had lifted my leg to step out on the sand when I swung it back around to stare at Kaity. "If your ancestors are in Maine, how does your magic work?"

She shrugged her shoulders again. "My mother told me that her family was extremely powerful, and that was the reason mine worked here. We've lived here my entire life."

That seemed strange, considering how far Maine was from Happy Valley, Oregon. But I didn't know that much about witches and their history.

"What kind of powers do you have?"

Kaity cocked her head to the side. "Hmm. Well, I can make fireballs like you." She paused, looking for confirmation.

I nodded.

"I can teleport across town as long as I've got a clear picture of where I'm going." She humphed. "I guess I've never really thought about it. Mother taught me about herbs and the healing properties they have. I usually spend Sunday brewing potions for sickness, concentration, or sleep." Her smile widened. "Oh, I can charm items." She banged her fist into her palm.

"What kind of things?"

"Broom, mop, vacuum, rags."

I laughed. "So, you're like a real-life princess."

She laughed with me. In between her giggles, she murmured, "I don't have an animal guide."

"Well, we'll find you one." I turned around to retrieve my arrows, laughing as I walked down the path.

"You like doing that?" Kaity asked when I got back. She came up beside me. "Could you teach me?"

I glanced her way before taking a deep breath in and releasing it.

"I can teach you, but with magic, wouldn't that put you at a disadvantage if you need to chant or something?" I asked, turning to see the three candles lit.

The wax melted onto the concrete. They would be good for one more session before I needed to replace them. Hopefully, the store would have more. *Why does it not feel like second nature yet? What am I doing wrong?*

"You're very hardcore," Kaity said beside me.

"What do you mean?"

"When you shoot, you look relaxed, but as soon as the arrow leaves the bow, your face gets this look."

I stood there waiting for Kaity to continue, but she looked more uncomfortable the longer I stared at her.

"What kind of face?" I finally asked.

"You know the one." She trailed off again.

I shifted on my feet. "Obviously I don't know, or I wouldn't ask."

Kaity huffed, "It's like you need to use the bathroom." She paused for a second. "Like your poop face."

I looked at her, a smile tugging at the corner of her lips. "I get it." And I laughed too.

"No, it's like you're afraid of your abilities."

That was the truth. "I . . . I burned down the chem lab at Berkeley when my powers resurfaced."

"You didn't?"

I heard the disbelief in her voice so I nodded. "Yes. Dad bound my powers when I was eight because they were so out of control at that age. But the time without them hasn't helped me learn to control them."

"How could you?" Kaity asked, leaning against a pole.

"That's true. I've had them for two and a half years now, and I feel like I've made little progress with them. Whenever I get angry, it bubbles to the surface, and I'm afraid I'll hurt someone."

"I've had mine my entire life, and my mother taught me growing up. I was homeschooled until freshman year because my mother wanted to make sure I had control of them," Kaity said.

"That must have been nice. My mother died when I was young, and there was no one else who could teach me."

She glanced in my direction. "Is that why your dad bound your powers?"

I nodded. "I think so."

"That must have been hard as a kid."

Yes. Not being able to manifest my powers turned into anger issues. I ran my hand through my hair. My fingers stuck in the braid I'd woven through it before work. "I'd always believed he had my best interest at heart."

"You don't now?" Kaity asked.

I shook my head. "I don't know. He won't answer questions about my mother. And it just seems weird that he won't talk about her."

Goose bumps peppered my arm. I tried rubbing, but the apprehension remained. My chest constricted as my vision dimmed a little. I found myself fiddling with the cuff's clasp.

"Ember?"

A voice filtered through the fog. I blinked several times to see Kaity standing in front of me, concern unmistakable in her eyes.

"Are you okay?"

What was that? I looked around. The aether telling me something? "I'm fine, but I'm exhausted. I think I need to go home."

Kaity stood silent a moment and then nodded.

As I picked up my gear, ready to go home, Kaity hesitated before climbing into the vehicle.

"What is it?" I asked, leaning against the car door. I looked across the top of the car toward Kaity.

"Do you want to come out with me tonight? I'm scheduled to go with one of the guys, but I'm trying a new spell that I'm not sure will work." She paused, eyes locked with mine, before she spoke again. "It'll be easier with you than with them. They want results."

I didn't answer right away, and I saw her eyes drop, determining I was saying no. Hannah was gone. I needed to find her and make sure no one else was taken. This deep desire that supernatural beings and humans could live in harmony resonated with me.

"Yes, what time?" I said finally.

Kaity's surprised look made me smile.

"Oh, like eleven, and I can meet you downtown."

I nodded to her and climbed into the car. Eleven would work.

Sixteen

EMBER

The cool night air made the hairs on my arms stand as I crossed the front lawn, practically running toward my car that I parked farther down the road. Dad had stayed awake later than usual, asking me questions about archery practice. While I enjoyed telling him about my accomplishments in that area of life, the drive downtown would take ten minutes. And my watch already showed eleven. I was late. *Hopefully she would wait for me.*

I pulled into a parking spot. This part of the city held older buildings, including the bank. The town square was deserted at this time of night except for a lone figure. *But would it stay that way?* As night continued, would we encounter more vampires? I wasn't sure how long Kaity and I would be out tonight, but having my gear with me eased my mind. I crossed the lawn with my bow and arrows strapped to my back.

"Hey," the dark figure yelled as I got closer. "You look like you're ready to hunt." Kaity came into view.

"Hey, sorry I'm late."

"Don't worry. I know a lot about sneaking out."

"Why do you think I snuck out?"

She smiled and headed off.

"But I didn't sneak out." *I just didn't tell my dad I was leaving.* I shrugged my shoulders and followed. "Where are we going?"

"One of the missing women owned a shop here, Jean Crafts. I'll do the spell there," she tossed over her shoulder.

We crossed the street and stopped in front of the shop window. Jean Crafts took up the entire front window in pale-blue cursive lettering.

"What kind of spell are you doing?"

Kaity looked around. Tugging the bag off her shoulder, she headed down the alley, out of view. "It's a location spell, but I've added another pillar to tell whether she is alive or dead."

"That's morbid but creative," I muttered as she pulled things out of her bag.

"It's how I found Luke after he disappeared from the hospital. I did a more simplistic location spell with one of his shirts he left at my house," she said, looking at me and instantly turning pink in the face.

I waved her off, and she continued to pull things out of her bag.

The lane was lit by one overhead light underneath the backdoor of Jean Crafts. It barely gave enough light for the door, let alone the alley. I leaned against the brick building, waiting for Kaity to get started. *Would Hannah and the rest of the missing girls still be alive once we found them? Would we find them?*

I watched as Kaity sat on the uneven brick road, feet under her as she set a bowl in front of her. She pulled out a group of iris flowers, holding them over the bowl. Her eyes closed, she held the flowers tight in her hand, perfectly horizontal as her chest rose and fell.

She touched the pendant that hung around her neck. Her eyes shot open, and she snapped her fingers, creating a single flame. Lighting the flowers, she waved them slowly, fanning them over the bowl, cleansing the surrounding air before the burning twigs dropped into the bowl. Opening a bottle, she trickled a few drops of liquid into the bowl before she closed her eyes again and chanted.

Mist rose from the bowl, swirling up as her voice grew louder. The chant ended, and the mist swooshed to the street. And nothing happened.

"Darn," Kaity cursed. "Glad I brought extra ingredients." She started the ritual again.

Ligatus et ligatus vide aspectum audite sonitum quod perierat nunc est inventus ligatus et ligatus.

Ligatus et ligatus vide aspectum audite sonitum quod perierat nunc est inventus ligatus et ligatus.

Ligatus et ligatus vide aspectum audite sonitum quod perierat nunc est inventus ligatus et ligatus.

Ligatus et ligatus vide aspectum audite sonitum quod perierat nunc est inventus ligatus et ligatus.

Dircum me quid peto tandem motus eius ostende nobis.

I leaned against the hard surface listening to Kaity chant words I didn't understand, but the language sounded hypnotic and pulled me in. There were several attempts. I stopped counting after a few, but finally, the mist swooshed down, and a red light appeared. It floated above the bowl, rising higher as it went to the middle of the alley.

"What is that?" I said, snapping out of the trance.

"It will track her last steps. I'm hoping that it'll show us what happened."

I glanced between Kaity and the light floating in the alley. It hovered for several minutes. Nothing happened. Then the ball zipped around the alley. As if it searched for something.

A bright red light flashed before my eyes.

As I lowered my arm, I gasped at the picture before me. Two dark figures stood in the alley with a smaller figure. It reminded me of Peter Pan's shadow. I tiptoed closer, and a hand came out in front of me. I turned to look at Kaity.

"Hold on. It'll show us."

And it did. The image showed a small figure, most likely Jean, fleeing to the safety of the shop. She wasn't fast enough before one of the larger figures grabbed her by her hair. Jean fell to the pavement. She stayed down, stunned. The dark figures moved toward her and pulled her to her feet. They dragged her deeper into the alley.

Kaity and I watched as the dark figures kidnapped

Jean. The image seemed lifelike; I shivered as I remembered my own attack.

In the back of the alley, one of the shadows let go of Jean. He moved to the wall, and to my surprise, the wall opened. A secret passage. Jean must have realized the danger of going into the wall. She kicked off the other attacker and fled down the alley. Kaity and I stepped back against the brick as her shadow passed us. Jean rushed by frantically as one of the dark figures sprinted after her. He caught her quickly and cut her off. He dragged Jean back toward the wall. In one smooth step, he pulled her into the darkness.

I stepped away from the building, my eyes on the spot where they had disappeared.

A look of lost hope was written on Kaity's face. "They went through there."

"That's not possible."

Kaity stood in front of the wall that the kidnappers had opened. Now that we knew where to look, we pressed against the brick, and the darkness opened to us.

"The light went inside. It'll show us the rest."

I didn't want to see the rest. "Is she alive?"

Kaity stepped over the threshold and looked back at me. "This magic is new to me, but I believe this means she's alive. Come on, the light is fading."

I nodded. *I can do this, just step into the hole in the wall.* One step later, and I was in the darkness. Two steps later, nothing had attacked us. Kaity formed a ball of light in her right hand, and I created a ball of fire in my left as we followed the red floating light. It reminded me of a haunted house I'd been forced to attend with Nessa. That had been a *strain* on my abilities.

We walked for several minutes in silence as we followed the faded red light. The tunnel led down, possibly into the storm drains under the town, and then headed straight. Several times, we came to a connecting tunnel. We would stop, thinking we would need to go back, then the light would brighten, and we would start tracking again.

"Where does this lead?" Kaity whispered beside me.

The red light zipped through the tunnel, giving it an eerie lighting. We traveled through the brick and steel until we met stone and dirt. Goose bumps had made a permanent home on my arms.

"I don't know," I said. "Did you know these tunnels existed?" When she didn't answer, I glanced over at her. She nodded. "Are they part of the storm drain?"

"No, these are older. Maybe built with the original town. There is one that connects with Parker though I've never used it. The bartender uses it to get around during the daylight."

"And Luke?"

"I believe he uses them too. He'll be pissed that the vampires are using it, and he didn't check here before."

I stopped as I listened to the sounds coming from ahead of us. The light hovered directly in front of us. A doorway led off from the main tunnel. I knew we had found something. The noises were faint but sounded like women. There were lower-toned echoes off the cave walls, which sounded like cussing.

I took a few steps through the archway, letting the fire die. We passed underneath it, and the red light faded. We stood on a ledge above a massive cave. Below us were several vampires and a group of women huddled together in the middle.

The cavern was shaped like a ballroom, almost like something had carved it. Vampires were posted along the sides of the rocky walls every ten feet. There were at least forty on watch.

"Oh my," Kaity whispered beside me. "Luke needs to know."

Before I could say anything, a bright blue light appeared beside me, and Kaity disappeared. I turned back to scan the faces of the women. *Hannah, where are you?* There. She was hunched over like the rest. I couldn't see her face from here, but her chest rose and fell. She was alive. *Alive.* I started back the way I had come, but when I turned toward the exit, a cocky smile greeted me. *Titan.*

"Well, look what we have here. The one that got away."

Seventeen

EMBER

My face slammed against the hard surface of the cave. Sand flew up. I blinked rapidly, trying to clear my eyes. I slid into one of the women huddled in the middle of the cave. My bow and arrows clacked against the floor somewhere out of my reach. I twisted into a crouch to face the vampire that had tried to kidnap me several days before. A vicious smile plastered his face.

Before I could summon fire to the surface, the cave shook. I landed on my knees as winds swept across the room. A giant light appeared off to my left. *Was it Kaity?* It grew to the size of a small vehicle. It flickered, then the haze cleared. A room lay beyond. Bookcases filled to the brim. *A portal.* A man strolled out toward us.

"Is that it?" he chimed.

I pushed to stand, gaining a good look at the person that must be in charge. He wasn't a vampire. His skin was a dark green. He wore a dark blue suit and tie with his hair slicked back. A demon, like Bob, but somehow, he felt more menacing than Bob could ever be. His red eyes scanned over me and turned back toward the other vampires. His life force matched the attacker from the park. This is the guy that killed Cliff to stop him from telling us everything.

Kaity left only seconds ago to tell Luke about the missing women. I hoped they were quick in returning as I eyed the vampires circling us. I glanced back at the group of girls. Eight women were huddled together. Dirty. Holding hands, heads down, their faces were bruised and bloody. *How long had they been here?*

Hannah sat at the back, her expression blank as she stared at me. *What had these women gone through?* I clenched my fist. No one deserved this. I found Jean next. Her face bruised purple, lip busted, but the fury in her eyes gave me hope. They were alive and could heal. These women were not broken.

"Who are you?"

I turned my anger toward the demon. "Who are you?" I took a step closer, hands clenched at my sides as I locked eyes with him.

He laughed. "You think you can save them all by yourself?"

He didn't know I'd come down here with someone else. That Kaity went for help. That I would burn them all alive to save Hannah and these women.

He stood there, his smile mocking me. The urge to wipe it off his face consumed me. The air around me heated as sparks extended from my fingers. I could do this. *I am in control.*

Lyra's guidance filled my thoughts.

I wanted the demon to burn for what he did to these women. And for the first time, I let the chaos take over, not reining the fire within me.

An inferno erupted around the women and me, also enclosing the demon and a few vampires in its circle. The monsters scattered, trying to escape the flames, but they weren't fast enough as the ring completed. They turned their attention to me. Some were wary, but others seethed.

The first few that stepped close died in the wave of fire as I motioned with my hand. The few remaining turned their attention to the helpless women. I closed my fist, and flames erupted from below them, turning them to ash.

The demon smirked at me.

The circle around us flickered.

Before I could take a step closer to the demon, a bright light flashed inside the cave. Kaity and Luke blocked my path.

Luke stood in front of me, facing the demon, a stake tucked in his back pocket. "Help Kaity with the women," he called over his shoulder as he sprinted forward.

I eyed the demon one last time, fist clenched as the flames flickered all around.

Kaity fought with the remaining vampires enclosed in the fire. She held her palms facing out, and using a pushing motion, she flicked the vampires into the barrier. The flames turned them into ash.

A glint caught my eye, and I rushed over to my bow

and arrows. I slung the quiver onto my back and let instinct take over.

The enclosed fire died down, and the few vampires left took advantage. They grabbed for the closest women and dashed off.

I cut off the vampire to my right. He smiled at me, letting go of Jean.

"Run," I yelled.

Jean didn't hesitate as she took off toward the others.

Kaity ushered them toward one of the few cave openings.

Taking advantage of my distraction, the vampire got close enough to grab the bowstring. "You're mine," he said.

I yanked the bow back and let go. It collided with the vampire's face as I pulled out an arrow. He hissed as he threw the bow down. It skidded across the floor.

I plunged the tip of the arrow into the vampire's heart. He grabbed my wrist as I tried to pull it out. His nails dug into my skin, blood sprouted. His eyes widened as his mouth popped open involuntarily. His head lowered to my blood, but vampire dust flew into my eyes.

I wheezed.

"You okay?" Luke asked.

I coughed again and nodded.

Luke dashed off. He fought the demon, putting his boxing to use, landing a punch square in the demon's face. The demon recoiled, sliding on the loose sand of the cave floor. The demon hit the rock wall, extending his hand to balance himself against the stalagmite.

Luke blocked the demon's incoming punch. He used his momentum to push the demon's arm back. But the demon countered with a kick to Luke's gut, sending him flying back, doubled over.

I made my way over to Kaity, scooping up the bow. I helped gather the women together. "We need to get out of here." I glanced around. "Is this everyone?"

She shot another fireball at the remaining vampires who attempted to get close to our small group.

"Ember," Kaity screamed, waving her arms.

I turned to where she pointed. A vampire grabbed Hannah and headed toward the portal. It pulsed and swirled, as if it were alive. I needed to stop him.

"Luke," Kaity screamed.

I turned to Kaity. "Go. Take the women and get out of here."

She nodded, ushering them out with Jean pulling the ones still in shock.

I turned around. "Hannah." She was in a trance, sheep-like as the vampire tugged her along.

We stood in a triangle pattern. The portal at the top with the vampire racing toward it, and Luke to the right, fighting the demon. I stood on the opposite side, the cave entrance behind me.

I stepped forward, fingertips already sparking as Luke picked himself up off the floor. He rushed the demon, catching him in a choke hold against the cave wall.

"Master." The vampire now stood beside the portal, eyeing the demon.

I grabbed another arrow, notched it, and prayed that it would make it before they went through. I watched as the arrow soared through the air and hit its mark.

The vampire jerked.

Hannah, linked to the vampire, swayed with him as he grasped the arrow. The vampire's body began to disintegrate as he pulled the arrow from his chest.

I watched in horror as Hannah fell through the portal, eyes wide, with the remaining piece of the vampire still clutching the arrow.

The portal pulsed again, sending a gust of wind through the cave. The sand swirled around the perimeter. The aether that came from the portal was dark. Much darker than the demon's aether. I shivered as the portal collapsed in on itself.

Hannah's face falling through would haunt my dreams. *Where did she go? How do we get Hannah back?*

"No!" the demon roared.

I turned as the demon kicked at Luke's legs to break free of the choke hold. Luke stumbled back, and the demon punched Luke in the chin with such force it sent him skidding across the cave floor into a group of vampires.

The demon looked at me. "Do you know what you have done?"

Yes, I knew what I had done. I had lost an innocent woman. *My friend.* The demon stalked toward me. He knew where the portal went. He could open it.

I notched another arrow.

"Ember, we need to get out of here." Luke fought the

vampires, trying to break free of their grasp, but there were too many of them.

I released the arrows in rapid succession until they were gone. The demon managed to dodge each one by milliseconds as he advanced toward me.

Damn.

I needed to know where Hannah ended up. He would talk.

I swung my bow at his face. He caught it and yanked.

I let go.

Demon's red eyes widened as he tried to steady himself. I took advantage, swinging at his chin.

He stepped back, but not before grabbing the strap of my quiver.

I balanced myself as I unclipped it. Twisting out of the straps.

The demon seemed to expect this move. His hand came up, but fire erupted out of my fingertips as I parried.

The demon dodged my flames. Smirking, he dusted off the embers on his clothes.

"You're the girl!" he hissed.

"Where does that portal go?" I yelled.

I stepped closer, dangerously close. My head told me to run, but my anger had control. *I needed more.*

"Where is she? Where's Hannah?" I shrieked as a circle of fire erupted around us.

I glanced at the fire I hadn't meant to create as my lips turned up. He now had nowhere to go. *He'll pay.*

He stood in front of me, mimicking the smirk on my face.

That was a mistake.

He grabbed my hand and twisted it behind my back as he drew me closer. "Do you want to know where she went? Come along to find out," he whispered.

The words tempted me, but his voice was laced with danger.

I pulled back to punch him, but he grabbed my arm and pulled it behind me until his other hand held both of mine.

My body pressed against his. His soulless red eyes looked at me, a smile playing on his lips. I shuddered, and he laughed.

"Maybe I can keep you for myself," he said. "That is if you're not the one."

He leaned down.

I turned as his lips touched the soft flesh of my earlobe. I pulled back but couldn't move away. His hold tightened. Trapped. By him, by life, by Dad. Anger bubbled to the surface, feeding the embers, and time seemed to stand still as his eyes widened.

He realized his mistake.

He let go as he grabbed at something behind his back. But it was too late.

The flames funneled from within me. A glint of silver caught my eyes before the flames engulfed us.

The world tilted and darkened.

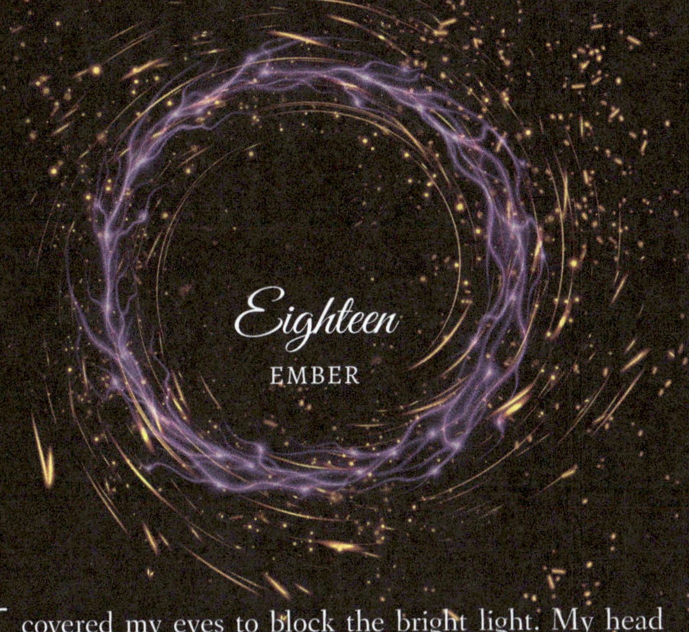

Eighteen

EMBER

I covered my eyes to block the bright light. My head pounded, vibrating like I was at a rock concert, but no music played. My limbs were heavy as I tried to move to a more comfortable position. *Why is this bed so hard?* Pain shot through my left side.

"Shh. Here, let me help you."

My eyes snapped open to the blue eyes of Christo Greyson. Questions assaulted my mind as I gawked at him. *Why was he here? How did I get home from the cave?* My heart raced as the room came into view. It wasn't mine.

Christo helped me turn onto my back before he stepped away from the bed.

"That's better, right?" he asked, a hint of a smile on his face.

Compulsion held me still. I couldn't help but stare. He seemed tanner, taller, and more ravishing than before.

He'd been decent at the bank that day. *He seemed . . . well hotter.*

He coughed to cover his laugh.

"I'm sorry," I started. "What happened?"

His grin grew. "There's time later for that. How do you feel?"

I stuttered, "My head throbs, and there's a pain." I reached down to point to my left side.

I pulled the shirt I was wearing—*this isn't mine*—and my skin was bright red. It was puffy around the white bandage extending from my left rib cage to the top of my hip. I peeled back the bandage to see stitches in my skin.

My pulse quickened, palms clammy, and I pulled myself into a seated position.

He moved to help, but I waved him off. It took a second to change positions with the least pain. I leaned my head against the bed, taking a deep breath, and looked around for the first time. *What the hell happened?*

The room was larger than any bedroom I'd seen before. The furniture reminded me of a department store showroom. *A rustic theme.* The walls, the pillows, and curtains matched. The curtains that hung over the two tall windows were a deep blue color giving contrast to the warm tan walls. A cabinet sat against the wall; I couldn't recall the name, but I pictured *Beauty and the Beast* clearly. The high ceilings had an intricate design of crown molding. The doors were made of solid deep cherry oak. *Was this a fancy hotel?*

"Where am I?" I tried again.

"My home," he said.

I waited for him to continue. "And where is your home located?" I voiced through clenched teeth.

He smiled. "In Whitehorse . . . Canada."

Canada. How the *hell* did I get to Canada? Awake, the aether swirled around the room. It brought back a mixture I couldn't quite place. Chris's signature differed from a normal human, but it was familiar. It didn't feel as dark as the demon in the cave, but they were alike. Panic rose inside me. *Chris was a demon. Was he a threat to me?*

"How?"

Why hadn't I noticed his energy at the bank that day?

He walked toward the window beside the bed, adjusting the curtain, allowing the sun in more. "I was in the cave when the walls shook. I thought an earthquake would trap me inside. Stumbling through the passages, I came to a cavern. It was all crumbling upon itself, but you laid there in the rubble."

"Was anyone else there?" Had Luke made it to safety? Did the demon perish in my fire?

He shook his head no.

"Why were you there?" The other demon and his vampire lackeys had been there to kidnap local women. Had he been a part of their group?

Was Hannah lost to me now?

"Trials," he muttered.

Trials? What did that have to do with Hannah?

Chris's eyes twinkled at me as he knew I hadn't been paying attention.

"What happened?"

He stepped closer to the bed. "You had a bit of a

tumble." His voice was level and slow. "The cave collapsed on itself; you rolled out of the debris. I caught you before a boulder smashed you."

"Thank you," I said breathlessly.

He'd saved my life. I was alive because of him.

"I was in the cave for my trials." He sat down beside me, laying his hand on top of my leg. Warmth seeped into my skin through the blanket. "You probably guessed I'm not human. My people believe in a coming-of-age trial."

"And your people are?" I jerked when a spasm caught me unaware. I clutched my side.

Christo gently pulled up my shirt again, examining the wound. "It looks much better today."

"I don't remember this happening," I choked as pain gripped me. *Why didn't I remember?*

Chris's touch on my bare skin tingled, and our eyes locked before he spoke.

"You were stabbed. Luckily it didn't go too deep."

I combed my memory for something to validate this. The demon didn't have a knife. Water clouded my vision, and the pounding started again in the back of my skull as I tried to filter through what had happened.

"You're okay. No major organs were hit. It'll heal nice. You might have a battle scar."

His widened smile gave me comfort that everything would be okay. A low beep sounded in the room. He pulled open the drawer on the bedside table, bringing out my phone. *Dad.* He would be frantic that I didn't come home last night. *Has it been longer?*

"How long have I been here?" I shrieked, plucking

my phone out of his hand.

He moved his hand back. "It's midmorning. It was late when I got us back here. We stopped at a healer before coming here. Probably around three or four this morning."

"Okay, it's not been a whole day yet."

I opened the phone to scroll through the missed messages and calls. Dad called several times, leaving voicemails each time he called. Luke had messaged me. *He made it out*! And then there were messages from Kaity and Grace. *Fuck*. I missed lunch with Grace.

"I need to call my dad and let him know I'm okay."

Chris stood from the bed. Several seconds later, the door closed. I leaned against the headboard studying the crown molding around the room. The demon had to be dead. The flames had to have killed him. If I had better control of my abilities, he would be alive. Was he the only one that could tell me where Hannah went? Would I be able to find her and bring her home?

I clenched my fist around the phone. Several deep breaths later, I organized my thoughts. What would I say to Dad? I needed a way around telling him what I'd been doing.

Thirty minutes later, I pushed the end button on my phone and opened a message to Vanessa. Hopefully, she would respond quickly. I sent messages off to Luke, Kaity, and Grace as I waited to hear from Nessa.

The door opened when a message chimed. The aroma of food floated toward me. I slid my phone under my leg as I closed my eyes, savoring the smell.

"I wasn't sure what you would like but started with soup."

Soup sounded good. It seemed like days ago that I'd eaten. My stomach gurgled in response.

"Thank you. What kind of soup is it?"

He set the lap tray down on the bed, and I could see that there were two bowls plus some bread. "It's a chicken and noodle base with some added ingredients."

I eyed him as he handed me the right bowl. The bowl was cool to the touch, but steam rose. I inhaled before dipping the spoon in. As soon as it touched my lips, the other secret ingredients didn't matter. It soothed my throat and somehow helped the heartache of losing Hannah.

"It's better with the bread dipped in," he said, dipping in his bowl.

I followed suit. The bread tasted homemade. I tore pieces off and dipped them into the soup, letting them soak in the broth before bringing it to my lips. The flavor of the soup had a hint of a metallic taste, which lingered before I washed it down with water.

After eating and having a conversation about how we both enjoyed living in Berkeley, I lay back against the propped-up pillows, my eyes closed.

"Why don't you take a nap. I'll wake you in a few hours."

I nodded at his suggestion and listened to him gather the dishes and head out the door. A nap sounded nice. I carefully slid back against the bed. I closed my eyes as warmth settled over me.

Nineteen

EMBER

When I woke the second time that day, sun slipped in through the curtains. The aether pulsed, confirming no one else was in the room. I reached to turn the lamp on, and as I moved, my leg bumped against my phone. I grabbed it. The screen showed it was two in the afternoon. I searched through the missed messages. None were extremely important.

I pushed myself into a seated position, and the pain came from my bladder this time. Three doors were in the room. The one Chris left through went to other parts of the house. A set of double doors reflected a rainbow through the glass onto the floor. The third door could be a bathroom or a closet.

I made my way slowly across the room. My feet turned to ice the instant they touched the hardwood floors. *Bathroom. Please, be a bathroom.* I twisted the knob to reveal a bathroom. *Jackpot.*

Walking back into the bedroom, Chris came in from the hallway carrying another tray.

We munched quietly on the toast he'd prepared. My eyes wandered to the furniture in an effort to avoid him, though they drifted every other minute. *Why was this so awkward? Did this count as our date we had planned?*

Christo coughed, gaining my attention from the wood grains in the bedside table.

"Would you like to stay another night?"

"I . . ." I didn't know if that would be a good idea. I needed to get home.

He smiled, and I fought the urge to leave my mouth hanging open.

"It would probably do you good to rest another night here before I take you home. While I can zap in and out of places, you may find it jarring."

Oh, he could teleport like Grace and Kaity. *I wish I could do that.*

"Um, so do you want to stay another night? Or at least stay most of the day. Take a nap or two," he asked again with his head tilted down. His eyes darted up quickly and then back at his black boots.

I nodded. It wouldn't hurt to be fully rested before going home in case I needed to deal with Dad. He thought I was in Berkeley helping Vanessa search for her lost dog. A dog she did not currently own. "I'll have to make a phone call."

He smiled, retrieved all the dishes, and left me to make that call. He called over his shoulder that I could use his shower and any clothes that would fit.

I searched my contacts and pressed Grace's name. It rang several times before anyone answered.

"Ehello?" a voice not belonging to Grace said.

I tilted my head. "Bob?"

"Yo, Ember," the bartender said. "They said you got hurt?"

"I'm fine. Is Grace there?"

"Nah. That girl's always leaving something in my bar. You tell her about it and she don't listen. Always popping in and out at all hours, thinking something's gotten to the boss man. Like anything could get to the boss man."

Grace checked in on Luke during the day? "Oh, can you tell her and everyone else I should be home tomorrow?"

"Sure can," he said. "I got more ingredients for a new margarita mixture if you're brave enough."

I smiled. "Um, I'll have to take a rain check." I paused, with nothing else to say. "Okay, bye, Bob."

Silence followed my goodbye. I pulled the phone down to see if he pressed end without saying bye, but the call was still ticking away. I hit the end button before the pain on my side panged from sitting like this. It had decreased since I first woke, but the slightest movements hurt. I lay down and closed my eyes as I started my meditation routine.

When I opened my eyes next, the light in the room had brightened. *Guess I needed more rest than I thought.*

I walked into the shower and washed the grime away. *Why didn't I do this sooner?* I stood sideways under the waterfall showerhead in an effort not to get the bandage wet, but having to reapply it seemed less important as the water trickled down my body.

After the shower, I searched for a comb but found none. Running my hands through my hair, I combed out the tangles as best as I could.

I stared at my reflection in the mirror, studying the dark circles under my eyes and the strain in my face. I was alive, but Hannah was still lost. I pounded my fist on the counter. I had made it through the fight with vampires and a demon. Exhilarating and scary at the same time. I would find Hannah. I'll figure it out. Maybe Kaity could do another spell.

The other problem I faced was at home. Would Dad find out that I lied to him? Grace had moved my car from the courthouse to her house for me. My two phone conversations with Dad didn't hint that he knew what I had been up to. He truly believed everything I had told him.

I wasn't ready to tell him everything yet. I needed more time and more information about my mother. If he would talk to me. Especially now that Hannah's life could depend on those secrets. I would need to decide whether I'd collect that pink box or stay on my course. I just hoped we found Hannah before it was too late.

"Ember," a voice called beyond the door.

Chris was back from wherever he had been earlier. The mirror told me I was decent. I headed back into the bedroom. Chris stood on the far side of the room with a tray in his hand.

"Would you like to eat outside? It's a little nippy, but not too bad." He noticed my wet hair. "Did you reapply the bandage? Let's do that first." He set the tray down on the end of the bed and motioned for me to sit down as well.

He pulled bandages from the side table, and I lifted my shirt as he applied a creamy mixture. As soon as his hands touched my exposed skin, a warm desire swirled deep inside. *Calm down Ember, he's just trying to help nurse you back to health.*

Our eyes locked, and I turned away, flushed. After what seemed like an hour, his hands fell away, and tightness sprang swiftly into my chest. Chris didn't seem to notice my reaction.

"Food?"

I nodded, rising to help him with the doors. I allowed him to go first. When I stepped out, the scenery took my breath away. The beauty of this place was extraordinary. I could see mountains in the distance with tops covered in white. Behind the house, a picturesque lake sat at the bottom of the hill. Every direction I turned, greenery surrounded me. The fresh air soothed my lungs as I took in a deep breath. My nostrils flared at the exquisite burn.

"This is beautiful, Chris." I sat in one of the patio chairs. He handed me a plate with a croissant on it.

"Turkey with cheese, nothing fancy but easy."

"Easy is fine with me. This place is breathtaking."

We sat in the quiet of the outside. The aether ebbed and flowed around the lush surroundings.

When I finished half of my sandwich, I asked to sate my curiosity, "What are you?"

He turned his head toward me with a raised brow. "What are you?"

My cheeks warmed at his rebuttal. "You go first."

He moved to face me, leaning back in his chair as he said, "I'm an Immortal."

"And that means what, exactly? You can't ever die?" Was there a listing somewhere for all the different types of supernatural creatures I could one day meet? If so, I really needed to get my hands on that.

He laughed. "No, we can die, but we heal much faster than a normal human." He paused, waiting for me to say something, but my head swam with more questions. "Ember, what are you? You can't be a human. You filled that cave with fire."

"Um, yeah, no, not exactly human. Half human, half Zodian."

He nodded. "I figured it was that or a witch."

I leaned back against my chair. I remembered what he said yesterday. "You were in the cave for a trial?"

He sighed. "Yeah, our people believe we become an adult at twenty-five, and to be accepted as full grown, each Immortal turning twenty-five has to go through a series of tests. The cave was part of one of those tests."

A test? What could he have possibly done down there? "What was the point?" I asked.

He shifted his body. "Not sure. They told us to go there and follow the signs. But when I arrived with two others, there weren't any signs that we could find. We ended up walking around for hours." He turned and smiled. "I should thank you. The cave collapsing gave us a reasonable excuse to leave."

I laughed. His smile deepened, showing off one dimple, and my chest constricted once more. "How many tests do you have to complete before you're accepted?"

"Not sure, but in a few months there's a party, and the regents will let us know if we passed."

"At least you have something to look forward to." I scanned the backyard when a breeze filtered through my hair.

"Um," Chris started.

I turned to look at him.

"Is it true that Zodians can create one element?"

"We don't create. We control the surrounding elements. They lend us their essence."

"And you can control fire?"

I nodded. "I'm half Zodian on my mother's side. She died shortly after my birth."

"That must have been tough. My dad died several years ago, and it's been hard on both me and my mother. I feel like I should live up to his legacy, which is why I didn't walk away from these tests that seem totally ridiculous now that I've described it to you."

Living with a single parent and trying to be what they wanted was tough. I didn't even know what my mother's legacy was. Mom didn't leave me on purpose, and while I know that Dad did the best he could, he was the one to bind my powers. It still hurt.

How strong would I be now if I'd grown up with my

powers and had the time to learn before being thrown into the midst of fighting? I knew I'd screwed that last fight. Would Hannah still be here if I hadn't unleashed my anger?

Meditate always. One of Dad's favorite lines.

The aether vibrated around me, and I found a flock of geese landing in the lake. Aether was the one element that seemed to work without focusing very hard. Fire had come naturally to me as well. Though it took a lot of focus, it flowed instantly, unlike the others.

"It's getting colder. Do you want to go back inside?" Chris asked as he hovered over me. I nodded, and he grabbed my half-eaten plate. "Not good?"

"No, not that hungry, I guess," I said and rushed to open the door for him, sending fresh pain to my side.

"Go slow, you don't want to tear one of the stitches and start bleeding again."

I nodded as I went in after him. Going to sit on the bed, I realized how tired the short walk had made me.

While Dad was probably okay with me staying another night since he believed I was safely ensconced at Berkeley, I did need to go to work tomorrow afternoon. There was no way Denise would take another shift since she'd already been filling in for Hannah.

I heard Chris leave as I tucked myself into bed. I fell asleep before he came back into the room.

I awoke to an empty room. The light dwindled behind the curtains. I stretched, glad that the pain was minimal. I checked my phone for any messages before getting out of bed.

A knock sounded as I came out of the bathroom.

Chris stuck his head in. "I was checking to see if you were awake and wanted to play a game before leaving?"

A game? "What kind?" I asked, trying to see the box behind his back, but the door hid it from view.

"The Game of Life." He laughed, bringing the box in front of him. "I was cleaning out a hall closet, and this fell on my head. I thought it would be a good send-off before you head back to the real world."

"Sounds good." I looked around the room for somewhere to play. "On the bed or the floor?" I pointed.

He sat on the bed. I moved to make myself comfortable as he set the game out.

An hour later, we were getting to the wire. It'd been years since I played. We would take breaks to discuss the game and real life. Chris discussed his father's unexpected death many years ago and one of the reasons why he went to Berkeley. A way to get away from everything. And now he was learning the family business. He didn't go in depth, but his body tensed when he spoke of it. He definitely didn't like the family business but didn't see a way out of it.

"That's cheating." Chris laughed as my car drove past the PhD spot on the game. "There is no way you picked that card." He reached for the card in my hand.

The heat startled both of us when our skin touched.

My eyes locked with his. He leaned closer, his hand wrapped around mine, pulling me toward him.

"So beautiful," he whispered before his lips crushed mine.

The game crashed to the floor, distracting me for a minute before his mouth found mine again. He pulled me closer to him. Heat radiated from his body. It drew me in. My hands acted on their own, skimming his body and lifting his shirt over his head.

What the hell *am I doing?*

His hands roamed my body, careful to avoid my bandaged side. We broke apart as he pulled my shirt above my head. He smiled as his eyes roamed over my body. I smiled, tugging him toward me.

He whispered against my lips, "Are you sure?"

I nodded. "Mmhm."

We sunk into the covers of the bed. The fading light reflected off our bodies.

I awoke much later, the room dark. My side burned. While he had been careful not to put weight on my body, the movements had aggravated it. Determined to find some pain reliever, I swung my legs off the bed. To avoid disturbing Christo, I left the light off. Hopefully there was a bottle in the bathroom.

"Top shelf," a muffled voice came from behind me.

I turned in the dark to stare at the lump in the bed. "Chris?" I asked.

He laughed. The lump moved, and a bright light blinded me. "Who did you think it was?"

Not liking the sarcasm in his voice, I answered, "You said top shelf? Top shelf for what?"

He sat up in bed, covering his lower half before responding, "The pain reliever is on the top shelf?"

I fumbled. "Pain pills, top shelf. How did you know?"

How could he possibly know that was what I was looking for? Had I spoken aloud?

Now, with the light on, I realized I stood naked in front of him. His eyes locked on me until I dove to get the sheet pulled around me. *Where did my clothes go?*

"Let's get dressed . . . Or we could get back in bed?" He smirked, sitting on the edge of the bed, letting the covers droop a little.

I dropped the pair of sweatpants and turned back to him. "How did you know I was thinking that?" I asked slowly. *This was super weird.* I could see it in his face. His eyes wouldn't keep contact. He knew what was going on. "What is it?" I spoke louder.

"Let's put some clothes on, and I'll tell you."

He climbed out of bed, his naked backside distracting me from his words. When he fastened his pants and turned back around to me, did I realize what he said?

"What's going on, Chris?"

"There is no easy way to say this . . ." He paused again, and I wished I could make him talk faster. He finally continued, "I can read your mind."

That wasn't what I thought he would say. Not sure what I thought he was going to say, but reading my mind hadn't occurred to me. *Could other people read minds? Or just his people.*

"I'm sure there are other creatures out there that can read minds, my people being one of them."

"Stop doing that," I yelled.

My sheet came undone, and I rushed to get my

sweatpants on and found my shirt half tucked under the bed.

"I'm sorry. It's new. I don't know if I can turn it off."

New. Reading minds was new to him. He said his people could do it. And like before, I didn't need to ask my question to have him answer it.

"It's new because of the ritual bond."

I became laser focused on him. "Ritual bond? What are you talking about?"

He sighed.

It stung as my nails dug into my palms.

"I found you in that cave, bleeding. I was afraid you were going to die."

"But you brought me to a healer. I remember you saying that." My foot started tapping against the hardwood floor.

"Yes, and we both agreed that your injuries were too severe to survive."

"But look here"—I opened my arms wide—"I survived."

He frowned at my display. "Only because we did the ritual bond."

Those words. Ritual bond. I knew it would be my undoing. "What the fuck did you do?"

He licked his lips. "It's a ceremony in my culture that binds two people's souls together. By doing this, they can send energy to the other. Help heal them."

Binds two people's souls together. *This is wrong.*

I stiffened; my vision blurred as the words swam

around my head. Betrayal. Lied. The irony was not lost on me.

Chris stood on the other side of the bed, big open eyes staring back at me. Wanting me to accept him. To tell him what he did was okay.

How could you? This is not okay.

I didn't know how this would affect me long-term. Would I have to tell my dad? I swayed, catching the side table to stabilize myself.

"It'll get better," Chris said, shrugging his shoulders. "You'll eventually read my mind."

"I'll read your mind . . ."

He smiled.

"How does that make it right?" I asked.

He faltered.

"How could you do this? Don't I have to agree?"

His face told me the answer. Yes, I had to agree, but he'd gotten around that. I wanted to stomp around the room and stab his face, but I didn't have a knife.

"How?" I demanded, coming around the bed to stand in front of him.

"The healer completed the ritual. You said yes when we were there."

A place I didn't remember.

"And then the bond takes hold after the couple . . ." He stopped talking, the tips of his ears turning red, and he gestured toward the bed.

"You gotta be fucking kidding me!" I shouted, backing toward the double doors. "I thought I was getting a piece of ass, not a fucking nightmare."

"Soulmate," he whispered.

I looked at his face, seeing the words hurt him, but I couldn't care now. He tricked me. "Did you have sex with me just to complete your ritual?"

"If we didn't complete the bond, you could have died. I decided earlier that I wouldn't complete the bond unless you agreed." He ran his hand through his hair, ruffling the blonde waves. "And you did." He grinned, his pants riding low with no shirt covering those taut sweaty abs.

I needed to get out of here.

"Don't leave," he shouted, lunging for me, but I turned sharply, darting out of the door, ignoring the shooting pain in my side.

"I thought it was just sex," I screamed as I sprinted off the patio to the green field beside the lake. The sun's dark reflection showed it dipping into the night sky.

I ran as fast as I could against the harsh wind. If I could make it to the high point in the field, I could see the surrounding areas. I could get away.

"Ember, don't leave," came his voice, muffled by the wind.

I jerked as lightning struck around me. A storm now? There had been no clouds in the sky? *Damn the weather.* Could this day be ruined any further? My brain told me to turn around and to go back. He was sorry. He tried his best. He would be better. I needed to flee the impending streaks of lightning. It took all my willpower to push through the lightning storm. *I had to get away.* Make it to the middle of the field. From there I saw no other houses in the area.

Trapped here with a liar.

Why did that seem to describe my life?

"Ember."

"Go away!" I screamed, holding my chin high, exposing my neck to the danger around me. Lightning bolted a few feet.

I am done being trapped.

Violet light engulfed me, and darkness followed.

Twenty

EMBER

What happened? My back ached as I climbed to my feet. A horn blared close by, and white lights flashed. I blocked my eyes as I tried to determine my location.

A car stopped before hitting me. "Move, ass!" the driver yelled.

I turned in circles, trying to get my bearings. I spotted Parker Elementary. I dashed off the road toward my home away from home for the past few weeks.

Happy Valley? The lightning had rained down around me. *How was I even alive?*

"Ember?"

Luke stood before me, his eyes locked on mine. His arms open—waiting.

What had I done? Christo was a fucking liar.

"Are you okay?" Luke said as he wrapped his arms around me, pulling me into his warmth. "What happened?" His eyes searched the surrounding area as he guided us to the doors.

Shame washed over me at the thought of Christo's deceptions. I couldn't tell Luke how stupid I was. *No!*

"Ember?" Luke repeated.

I snapped back to the present as he pulled open the front doors of the school, ushering me inside. Instead of turning left into the cafeteria, we swung right down the dimly lit hallway that led to the maintenance room Luke called home.

"Sorry," he muttered.

He flipped the light switch. A bed sat tucked under the only window, which was spray-painted black, with a small end table. It was a decent size, but they were the only contents of the room. He gently led me to the bed.

"Whatever happened, we'll figure it out, but you need to tell me."

"I'm okay now," I croaked out as I tried to keep the tears at bay.

His hand lifted slowly, as if he was afraid I would bolt like some skittish mare. I held my breath as he wiped a tear off my stained face. My life had turned upside down. I'd stepped foot in the supernatural world. A world Dad didn't want me to be in. Was this my punishment for not drinking the elixir? Wanting to know more about my mother? *For wanting to be myself?*

He brought his hand down and laid it on mine. "I'm here if you need me. No judgment."

I glanced at his warm chocolate eyes, which had

always had the power to hold my attention. *Distraction.* "How are the women?"

He leaned back. "We took them to the police station."

Air rushed into my lungs. I hadn't realized I was holding my breath. We'd saved those girls.

"What about the magic they saw? Will they be okay?" *They had been through so much.*

"Kaity wiped their memories of us, our battle, and made them believe they freed themselves."

Good. Lowering my head into my hands, I took a long deep breath. *What the hell was I going to do about Christo?* I knew Dad and the others couldn't find out how much trouble I'd landed myself into. Not yet. Hannah still needed to be found. And I needed to know all my family's secrets.

The electricity still ran through my veins, making me twitchy. Unable to sit still, I jumped to my feet, Luke watching as I paced back and forth.

I recounted the last seventy-two hours in my head. Could I have changed anything? *No.*

I stopped in the middle of the room. I wouldn't have done anything differently, given the opportunity. Kaity's spell would have still led to the same cave.

"Ember?"

I tilted my head to see his features soften as I held his gaze. He offered me a small smile, and my defenses collapsed.

"I feel trapped, Luke." My voice was barely above a whisper, but I knew with his hearing, I didn't need to be any louder. "I'm sorry I left."

He stood, taking a small step toward me.

My hand went up to halt him. I needed to get this out; the words had waited too long to come out. "When I left . . ." My fingers clenched at my sides. "I know I hurt you. I chose the path my dad laid out for me. As a child, I was told stories. I barely remember having powers before they were locked away, but I know what it's like not to have them. I'm not proud that I left you in the courthouse that day."

"You were there?" He cut in.

I nodded. "I arrived late, but my dad caught me in the hallway. He told me . . ." I licked my dry lips to wet them. "He told me I would be putting *you* in danger."

He moved to my side in a blink of an eye. He touched my lower back. "You shouldn't have had to choose alone. I would have respected your wishes. We would have found a solution together."

His face was inches from mine. I knew he meant every word, and I had robbed him of that choice.

"I'm sorry. It was wrong of me to make those kinds of choices for you. I should have told you what I was and let you decide for yourself."

He wrapped me in his arms. "It's okay. I'm here for you now."

I pressed against his chest, and he stepped back once more.

"It was the right decision for me at the time. I was going from being Daddy's little girl to your wife. Never having the opportunity to find myself. Berkeley helped me do that. And now I'm back here, and all those years of being little-miss-perfect is crushing me. Suffocating me."

He reached for me again, and I leaned into his embrace.

I glanced at his face. "I had planned on calling you after I left, but I was already halfway there when I realized my phone was missing." His face tensed. "I understand why you're still mad."

He spoke softly. "I was mad then, but not at you."

I'd disappointed him. That was worse, but I knew deep in my soul that going to Berkeley had been the right choice.

We stood in the center of the room, holding onto our lost memories.

"It was my fault."

The words were so low that I didn't think I heard them correctly. I peered at his face. "Your fault?" I questioned.

He looked away from me before answering. "My parents' death."

"Grace told me it was a car accident. You're not responsible for that."

He shook his head and pulled out of my arms, the cool air replacing him. He sat down on his bed, his head in between his knees. "We left before the sun rose."

I moved to the bed and sat beside him. I laid my hand on his back, encouraging him to continue.

"When the sun rose that morning, I had my first reaction to the sun. It was hot and blistering. It was excruciating. I'd fought against the belt holding me in the sunlight. It distracted my dad, and he lost control of the vehicle."

He lifted his head, his eyes haunted, staring through me, reliving the accident. I wondered how many times in the last two years he had revisited these moments? Too many to count, I'd bet.

"It was my fault," he whispered again.

Grace never told me how he became a vampire. But if he reacted to the sun that morning, he had been turned into a vampire before.

"I didn't know what was happening. I was fine the day before. Excited to be twenty-one." His voice was low as he spoke.

"Nothing strange the day before?" *How did he turn into a vampire and not remember it?*

"No." He closed his eyes. "I met a Shaman in North Dakota a few months after it happened. He told me that sometimes the actual event is too painful to remember."

It seemed strange. "You're not cold," I said, spitting out something I didn't understand.

"What?"

"You're not cold. Your body isn't like the other vampires. When those two vampires jumped me, their body temperature was freezing, but you. You feel like a regular person."

"What does that mean?" he asked

I shook my head. "I don't know. Are there different kinds of vampires?"

"Your body temperature has always felt hotter than normal," Luke said absently.

I smiled. "That's because I have fire running through my veins."

He smiled, but I could tell I hadn't convinced him the wreck wasn't his fault. I didn't know how to help his grief. I'd grieved for things I didn't have. He grieved for everything he lost. Luke ordered me to lie down and rest. Then told me he needed a drink and left.

When I woke, I knew I needed to head home. Luke let me borrow his truck to drive out to Grace's house to get my car. And it was on the drive that I realized my phone was back at Chris's house and my keys had been in my jeans during the fight. And only he knew where they were.

I pulled into Grace's driveway and saw my car parked by the barn. After turning off the engine, Grace walked down the steps from the house.

"Hey, thank you, thank you," I yelled, grabbing her for a hug.

"You're welcome, but you have to tell me what happened."

I sighed. Even after spending some quiet moments with Luke, thinking and mulling over what had happened, I wasn't ready to talk yet. "I will, but not now. I need to get home. It's almost one in the morning."

"Yeah, that's what happens when you go off on your own and don't keep in contact with your friends." Grace handed the spare key that always hung in the entryway of Dad's house.

"How did you get this?"

She rolled her eyes at me. "I popped in and popped out. It's not like I'm gonna hot wire your car."

"Oh, wouldn't you use your powers?"

She laughed like I had shared a joke. I squinted. *Why was she laughing?*

"I can't carry a large item or it drains my powers."

That made sense, in a way. The more power I used, the more tired I got. But the more I practiced, the less tired I would be. A mental and physical workout.

"Thanks for doing this."

"I'm glad you're okay." She hugged me again. "When Kaity tried to explain what happened, I had a hard time imagining that you would be okay."

"I'm okay," I said, squeezing her arm before releasing. "Seriously though, thanks for getting my car. If Dad found out that I was practicing and everything else." I shook my head, trying not to focus on Dad's anger. I had my own to deal with.

Grace gave me a look.

"What?"

"You need to tell your dad. It's not like he's in the dark about this world. Not like my parents. They are blissfully happy not to know any of this supernatural stuff."

"It's not the same. Yes, Dad knows this world, but he doesn't want me to be a part of it. He thinks it's danger-ous. And of course, he uses my mother's death to rub that in."

My own words weighed heavy. *Would he ever be*

okay with all of this? A bullfrog broke through my concentration. I needed to get going.

"Luke said he would pick up his truck later. I left the keys inside it."

Grace nodded, waving as I left.

Twenty-one

EMBER

I opened the door as quietly as possible. I didn't plan on being this late, but after the mad dash from Chris and spending time with Luke and Grace, it was unavoidable. Shit happens. *Dad would be asleep anyway.*

I tiptoed through the dark house. The hallway light seemed brighter than normal. Ever since I was a child, Dad would leave a dimmed light on in the hallway where the single picture of Mom hung.

A shadow danced. I stopped and backed farther into the darkness.

He's awake? From the street, the house had seemed quiet. I squatted behind one of the dining room chairs to get a better view.

Dad knelt on the floor with his back to me, a wooden box sitting before him. He held a swirl of silver over his head.

I covered my gasp with my hands. I'd seen that box before. I held still, waiting to see if Dad heard me. He didn't turn his attention away from the sword. My mother's sword. The sword that had brought them together.

He showed it to me years ago, but he wouldn't let me hold it. It was mine. It had spoken to my soul when I first laid my eyes on it. He kept it in a box in a locked cabinet all the time. I'd almost forgotten it was there.

Dad held the sword high in the air and then brought it back to his lap. He lowered it into the box.

Crap. I needed to move, or he would see me when he put the box back into the cabinet.

I backtracked to the kitchen. I cracked open the back door and shut it louder than before.

"Em?" Dad yelled from the hallway.

I waited a few seconds before answering him. Time for him to hide the sword. When I walked around to the hallway, he stood in the middle of it, facing the picture of my mother.

"It's late. You didn't have to stay up."

He smiled and embraced me. "Yes, I did. How was your trip? You're such a good girl."

Surprised, I wrapped my arms around him. *Weird.* His normal warmth was a pat on the shoulder and a smile.

"It went well. The drive didn't seem as long as I thought it would," I said, hearing the truth in the words, as Grace's house was only ten miles from here.

"And Vanessa, is she doing better?"

I nodded, surprised he remembered my roommate's name. "Yeah." I pushed past him to the stairs. "Unfortunately, we didn't find her dog."

"That's sad. Who knows what grabbed a hold of it," he said matter-of-factly. He turned, likely headed to his room. "Good night."

"Good night," I returned and took the stairs two at a time.

I entered my room, not bothered by the darkness, and plopped onto the bed. Glow-in-the-dark stars gleamed from the ceiling as I pictured my mother's sword again. I doubted Dad would hand it over willingly.

Steal it. Where did he keep the keys?

The aether slithered up and down my arms, constricting around them. I rubbed them, coming to a sitting position, staring into the shadows at the intruder. *Christo.*

He stood in one corner, his body relaxed as he leaned against the wall. "Ember, we need to talk," he breathed.

"I have nothing to say to you," I hissed through the darkness.

His dark figure darted across to me. "I'm not going away."

"You are if I don't want you here," I said louder, and then realized Dad could still be awake downstairs. "You tricked me," I snarled each word at him.

He hesitated as the words sliced through the room.

Tired of the darkness, I reached to turn the lamp on. Chris stood bathed in the soft light. Distracted, my breath hitched at his beauty. He reached in to caress my cheek. I leaned into his warm palm. Awareness hit me. I glared and pulled back slowly.

He sighed and sat on the bed beside me. His eyes

closed for a moment before he took my hand in his. "I'm sorry. I've explained why I did it. It was unfair of me not to tell you what would happen. But I can't take it back. There's no way to break it."

Of course not. I yanked my hand out of his, the skin tingling from the contact. "There has to be a way. There's always a get-out-of-jail-free card."

He linked our souls together without my consent.

"I'm sorry," he said through gritted teeth. "We need to talk this through."

"What is there to talk about?" I hissed. "You lied. I need a way out."

I would not remain trapped anymore. Not by anyone.

"You're not trapped," he uttered.

"Stop reading my mind," I spat; spittle sprayed onto my hand. I rubbed it onto the sheet.

"Please." He leaned closer. "Let's discuss this. Don't shut me out because you're scared."

Scared? I was not scared of him. I was tired of living in everyone else's lies. I had to go behind Dad's back and was continuing to do so. I didn't want to see his disappointment in me. I'd seen that enough throughout my childhood.

Chris shifted on the bed, and I knew he'd read my thoughts. I chose to ignore it. There had to be a loophole.

"I don't know of any," he mumbled.

I closed my eyes and took a deep breath. We needed to find it. "Please, I don't hate you. I probably should for all of the lies. I just want to be Ember. Not tied to anyone. I don't need this added complication. I have enough in my life already."

He nodded. "I understand. I've grown up with rituals and procedures. The two years in Berkeley were the best years of my life. If I could, I'd go back, but I can't. I have responsibilities to my race. And one of them is this trial. There are trials I must complete in a few months' time to be worthy of my ascension. It's a ritual that will activate my immortal abilities, and I will gain strength." He paused, looking me in the eye for the first time in several minutes. "The last test is claiming a soulmate."

I leaned against the headboard. "That's part of the trials? A soulmate and you picked me? Why me?" I saw I caught him off guard. He turned his head, avoided my gaze, and I knew there was something else he was hiding from me.

"I don't regret saving your life. Compared to other girls at Berkeley, I could tell you had a kind soul."

"That doesn't answer the question."

I watched him take a deep breath. His hands reached for my right wrist where I wore my cuff bracelet. I never took it off. I tugged as he attempted to untie the laces.

"Chris." I tried harder to move out of his reach, but he clamped down on my upper arm to hold me still.

He flung the cuff behind him and released my arm. I stared down. It had been years since the last time I studied the mark of my heritage.

A birthmark kept hidden from the world.

A birthmark I didn't understand.

The only gift from my mother.

A mark that showed the world I was not normal.

Just a bunch of triangles fused together on the only patch of skin that was stone white. One large triangle with a smaller one in the center, making it look like a teepee. The golden color made the pattern glint in any light. Attached to the top half, two smaller triangles faced opposite directions. Both of them had tails that looked like a sideways T. A bar at the center linked them all together.

"I saw this," he drawled.

"What does it mean?" I whispered, tracing the lines.

The mark was relatively small, the size of an Oreo cookie. I'd never known what it meant. I wasn't even sure if Dad knew. He always told me to just keep it hidden.

His eyes softened. "It's the mark of the Zodian."

I rolled my eyes. "Yeah, I knew that."

His smile widened. "There are thirteen tribes of the Zodians. Each tribe has a unique symbol. This comes from the thirteenth. The royal bloodline."

"Royal bloodline." I'd never heard that phrase before, but that didn't surprise me. Dad didn't talk about my mother. My grandmother's stories were distant, mythical memories. "What does it mean?"

"How much do you know?" he asked and stood from the bed.

Christo wandered to the vanity. His eyes scanned the pictures tucked in the sides of the mirror. He pulled an old picture of Luke and me sitting on a porch swing.

"Who's this?" he asked as he flapped the picture in the air. Jealousy laced his voice.

I rushed out of bed. "It's an old friend." I plucked the picture from his hand and returned it back to the mirror. I glanced over the old photos of Grace and me before my attention went back to Chris. "And I don't know that much. I knew they lived in tribes, but I didn't know there were thirteen of them. I found one tribe outside of Berkeley, but they wouldn't let me in."

He stepped closer. "They've been in hiding for years."

I tipped my head back to look at his face. "Why?"

"The Fall of the Heavens," he said, like I should know what those words meant. He laid his hand on my shoulder gently. "The Chaos Brothers slaughtered the royal bloodline in the capital city eons ago and have been hunting them over the centuries."

The same brothers that were kidnapping women to find the Zodian Warrior. I stepped out of his embrace. The royal bloodline ruled the Zodians. It was all beginning to make sense.

I turned back to Chris. "How do you know all this?"

He cocked his head to the side. "It's common knowledge, and there are several immortals who were alive when the Fall of the Heavens happened."

"But that doesn't explain why you chose me?" I asked for a third time.

"I saw the mark and knew you would be powerful."

"Powerful?" I whispered to myself and snorted. Grace thought the same thing. I'd hardly proven myself.

"You traveled from my home to your home in a blink of an eye. That's power."

He was still hiding something from me. "What does it mean for you, though?"

He ran his hands through his hair. "I'm not a normal member of my race. I'm their prince, and with the last of the royal bloodline as my soulmate, we will be magnificent."

I laughed, covering my mouth as another snort came out. I read Christo's perplexed face. "Me? I'm a princess? Nah, no way." *He's crazy.* All he wanted from me was my power.

"What do you think the royal bloodline is?"

"Not a princess, and that doesn't mean I'm from that bloodline. It's not like the only people in the thirteenth tribe are royalty." Or at least I hoped.

The perplexed look didn't fade as he thought through the words I'd spoken. "No, I highly doubt as powerful as you are that you're some mere tribe member. You are the last reigning queen."

What the fuck? Reigning queen.

"It's true. There isn't a lot of knowledge about the royal family. Like I said, they went into hiding several centuries ago."

Madness came to mind to describe this conversation. *I can't be.* He had to be wrong.

He gave me a sharp look. "I'm not wrong."

"Whatever. You decided because of this mark to trust me with your soul. That's crazy," I said as I lifted the window a few inches to get some circulation into the room. The fan haphazardly made circles, but the room temperature rose with each lunatic word out of Chris's mouth.

"Let's stop trying to make jokes." He ran his hand over his face, scrubbing at the day-old beard. "Let's make the most of it."

I crossed my arms. "And how will we do that? I want out of this."

He sighed. "You want information on your people, correct?" he asked. "I can help you get it, but you have to make this relationship work." Hook, line and sinker. "We can't lie to each other. We would know the truth." He came to stand in front of me. "Generations ago, couples would get married without meeting, and some of those marriages resulted in happiness. Why can't ours be like theirs?"

Because this is not some cheesy romance.

Marriage. Soulmate. Green eyes flashed before me. Deep inside me, an ache started. I didn't know why. Until I figured a way out, there wasn't any reason to fight Chris at every turn. While it might trap me, I knew I would find a way out. He was far more willing to provide the answers I couldn't get from Dad.

I held out my hand to him. "All right, I'll try."

He took my hand and kissed it, tightening his hold and pulling me closer. I lost my footing, and he caught me against his hard body. His lips found mine. I pulled back enough to gain my balance. When he shifted his mouth, his tongue pushed inside.

Surprised, I opened further, allowing his tongue to mingle with mine, and heat pooled at my core. He tugged me harder against him. His nails dug into my skin, but I didn't seem to mind as his tongue ravished mine. I sagged against his body, molded into his. His fingers trailed across my back, tangling in my hair, as his body tightened against me.

He stepped forward, and the bed pressed against the backs of my knees. That small movement brought me back to myself.

I pushed against his abs in an attempt to break for breath, his skin burning. I was lost again.

One hand touched the back of my neck while the other roamed my breasts.

I stiffened. *What am I doing?* I retreated again when he dipped into the front of my sweats. I moaned into his mouth as his fingers found my entrance.

"You're wet," he growled. "You want me to fuck you." He twisted, and we fell onto the bed.

I landed on top, my legs straddling his erection naturally, my core seeking fulfillment. The quick movement broke the spell, and I tried to pry myself off him one more time. He flipped our positions and yanked at the sweats, trying to give him access to what he wanted. I moaned as his fingers worked inside me.

His mouth left mine as he traced kisses to my ear. His hand freed the hard length that pressed against my leg.

"Open for me." He demanded. He trailed kisses down my throat before capturing my lips.

His tongue sought entrance as he thrust into me. His lips muffled my gasp.

He pumped to the hilt and back out. His eyes closed,

lost in the sensation and rhythmic motion of our bodies. The sound of my wetness echoed with every thrust.

"Good girl," he whispered as he shuddered into me. He kissed me one last time before he stood. "I'll be in touch." And he was gone.

The tears began to fall before he'd fully disappeared. *How am I going to live like this?*

Twenty-two

EMBER

The next morning the heaviness in my chest was stronger than before. I sighed, clutching the covers and wishing I could crawl back under them and hide for the remainder of my life. I could practically hear Vanessa telling me how one-night stands were no big deal. That people could be adults after, but this thing with Christo was not that simple. I pictured his toned body leaning against the bedpost. A pang shot through my lower body, and I cleared my mind. *That's what got you into this mess.*

I rolled out of bed, still stiff from the previous night. The shower rained needles down on my sensitive skin despite the soothing heat of the water.

I went downstairs to find something to eat. Dad was sipping on a cup of coffee, reading a newspaper when I came into the kitchen. I attempted a smile, but he never looked up. I ground my molars as I walked over to the cabinet. When I reached for the box of cereal, he grabbed my arm, and I jumped, tugging my wrist free from his grasp. Cereal scattered across the floor. My heart pounded, and I laid my hands against my chest, soothing the panic as I met my dad's eyes.

We seemed to ignore each other's crazy reactions. His eyes were zeroed in. I followed the line of sight to see that my bracelet was missing. Christo had tossed it to the floor the night before, and after the tears ran dry, I fell into a fitful sleep forgetting it.

"Where's the bracelet?"

I brought my arm down beside me, annoyed, but he grabbed it, pulling it to him as he inspected the mark.

"Emma, the bracelet?"

Not liking his tone, I pulled my arm back and shrugged. "I took a shower."

He pointed to the hallway, his eyes darker than usual as he hissed, "Go put it back on."

I glanced in that direction. "Later," I said. "No one else is here anyway. Let's talk about Mom."

"What?" Confusion washed over his face.

"I want to talk about Mom. About how she's part of the thirteenth tribe." My hand came to perch on my hip. I narrowed my eyes, making contact.

"Thirteen?" he sputtered, taking a step back and breaking contact to look around the kitchen, almost like he would bolt at a moment's notice. Then I watched as the mask came down. He stood taller, and his eyes narrowed on mine.

"I'm not sure where you heard that, but you are incorrect."

I bit down on my bottom lip before I spoke again.

Had Christo been wrong? "Oh, so what tribe is she a part of then? She has to be part of one of them? There are only thirteen that make up the Zodian population. Which one, Dad?"

"I am done talking about this," he hissed, pointing his hand again toward the hallway.

I flinched at his words. *He was done?*

"Go put the bracelet back on. You can't show that mark to anyone. Ever."

"Why, Dad?" I asked, crossing my arms. "Why all the secrecy? It's part of *your* wife's history."

He stomped over to me, his face inches from mine. I took a step back. His eyes narrowed; splotches of red appeared on his neck. It had been ages since I had seen him this mad. The last time had been that small fire I created before my eighth birthday. The reason he chose to bind my abilities.

"Go to your room, and put that bracelet on. Now!"

"Or what, *Dad?*" I asked, "Gonna make me go without supper like I'm a little girl all over again? Or did you fail to see that I'm a fully grown adult now? I'm not a child anymore. The fact that you won't talk about Mom makes me think you're hiding bigger secrets than those I know about." I stepped back as tears surfaced and opened my mouth before closing it again. I continued once the tears were at bay, swinging my arms wide, asking, "What is it, Dad? What's the secret?"

He stood before me, his veins visible, his mouth tight, and a flush washed over his face more prominent than before.

"End of discussion." He stomped out of the kitchen.

Moments later, I heard his bedroom door slam shut.

I sighed. *Well, that got us nowhere.* I wouldn't let guilt consume me for what I'd asked. Those were easy enough questions. I stomped on the cereal and let my anger out. The pieces engulfed in tiny flames around me, lasting only a second, and they were gone before any damage could be done.

My anger had been cut loose. Christo had thrown everything out of whack. He looked so good, just like a perfect fondant-covered wedding cake, but the flavors *just* weren't there.

I darted for the back door taking the stairs two at a time as I sprinted away from the house. I gained speed the farther I got. But my mind replayed the fucking and fighting over and over.

Men are so frustrating. Why couldn't they just understand where I was coming from?

I tensed, taking in my surroundings. The graveyard. *Why did I come here?* I'd stopped at the dead soldier. The cavalry rider stood in the center of the cemetery, standing half the height of an average tree. The base color had faded over the years, but the detailed work of the carving showed the magnificence in the rider's strain as he faced an unseen onslaught. The skill was beautiful in a creepy sort of way.

"I hope he's not an ancestor," a voice came from behind.

I spun around to see the jerk from the bank. He was dressed in similar clothes, dark on dark.

"With that uniform, he more than likely slaughtered thousands of your people," he continued as he walked closer.

"*My* people?" I asked. Eager for a fight.

He stopped. "That was presumptuous of me."

"At least I know your rudeness from the other day is your normal state of being. I'll remember that," I spat and started to walk past him.

He blocked my path. I stopped short, my hands grazing the threads of his black jacket. He caressed my cheek, wiping away the suspended tear that held desperately to my eyelash. Warmth spread through me at that gentle contact.

"Ember, what's wrong?"

I stepped back from the contact and wiped my face free of the tears I'd cried during the run.

"I . . ." I started. His emerald eyes pierced mine, and I bit back my retort as I realized he knew my name. I took him in. All of him. Dressed in black, a tiny red cross on the sleeve. "Kitley," I uttered.

He grimaced. "Kit. Please call me Kit. I didn't think you recognized me at the bank."

I stepped closer. "I didn't. It's been a few years."

He laughed. "I think the last time I saw you, I helped you sneak back into your dorm room while you were telling me how beautiful I looked."

My face grew hot. "I was very drunk that night."

He shrugged his shoulders. "It was your birthday. I think we sometimes need a night to cut loose." He smiled.

We stood there looking at each other, grinning like idiots. *What is happening?*

But then he broke the connection as he glanced around the cemetery. "I didn't mean to intrude."

"You're not. Am I intruding? Are you meeting someone?" I asked.

He straightened, tensing. "Nothing like that."

"Ah. You're here to visit someone?" I glanced at the nearest headstone.

"Is that what you're here for?" he asked.

I shook my head.

We stood in the shadow of the statue, silent as the sun shone down around us.

"I . . ." I took a breath in and out. "I had a fight with my dad." My shoulders sagged with relief. Talking with Lyra wasn't usually helpful since she didn't understand, and while Grace and I had reconnected, she'd been busy lately with the Collective. Neither one really understood my desire to please my dad.

"Ah." He stepped even closer. "I've had to deal with that a few times myself." He wore a sad smile on his face.

"Sorry," I muttered.

His smile grew. "It's okay. It's been a while. Both my mom and dad are gone now."

"It doesn't make it hurt less."

He laughed. "I agree."

His laughter reminded me of crashing waves on a warm sandy beach. It eased the tension in my chest as his jewel-toned eyes amplified the sound that came from deep inside him.

"I'll show you my favorite spot."

His smile widened at my invitation, and he nodded. I led him to the back of the cemetery, to a tombstone with a bench. I sat down, and he sat beside me. His thigh touched mine, and I glanced over at him, a slight blush crept up his neck.

A fountain lay before us. It was placed on a round stone divided in fours. On one side sat a wooden windmill slowly turning despite the nonexistent wind. A tiny waterfall trickled water down into the next quardrant containing dirt and flowers. The other side held a candle. The flame danced to the sound of the water. I'd never seen the flame extinguished.

I found this little spot a while back during patrol one night. Luke had run off in chase of vampires that moved faster than I could ever dream. I had waited on the bench for Luke to return. It hadn't been long but enough time for me to take a breather.

Sometimes I would think about the person who lay below the surface. How beautiful a soul to have deserved such a masterpiece above the soil. Perfect harmony of the four elements.

I brought my hand up, wanting to connect to this piece, no bigger than a standard shipping box, but the slight touch against my leg made me put my hand back down.

"It's beautiful," he said beside me. "Do you know who is laid to rest there?"

"Nope."

He chuckled. My stomach tightened at the sound.

"Did you—"

"Yep," I cut him off. "I've checked the tombstone for a name every time I pass by this place. There's no writing on it."

I felt his stare, so I turned to look at his raised eyebrow.

"I walk through here on my way to . . ." *Patrols.* "Work," I finished.

"This is way better than the rider," he muttered beside me. "So do you sit here often," he asked, "when you have a fight with your dad?"

I looked out over the cemetery, listening to the fountain, soothing my soul from the fight. "No, usually I grin and bear it."

"Ah," he said. "I did that as a kid, but I kept having the same recurring nightmare." He paused to take me in.

I could tell he wasn't really looking at me but experiencing the nightmare. I stayed still for as long as he needed.

"Of drowning, and after a while," he continued before pausing again. "After lots of therapy and other remedies, I told my parents they were no longer happening."

"But they were?" I finished for him as I placed a hand on his knee.

He graced me with a grateful smile and nodded. "Do you think maybe you can patch it up with your dad?"

I removed my hand. I honestly didn't know at this point. He was keeping too many secrets from me. I think maybe Chris might be my only option—sex in exchange for answers.

Kit's knee nudged mine when he stood. "You seem to have a lot to think about." He stared off but turned back around. "See you soon, Ember."

"Bye," I whispered as he walked away, taking a piece of me with him.

Twenty-three

EMBER

How many times had I called Lyra over the last month? I set my phone on the concrete table in an attempt not to hurl it into the tall grass around the range. I'd plastered her inbox with urgent messages. I huffed. *Why was she like this?* She would be available to talk for several weeks and then would disappear off the radar.

A month had passed since that fateful *soul* mating with Chris. I wasn't any closer to a solution there. I'd seen him a few times since. Each time started fine but ended with sex. *Glorious, defined sex.* My face heated at the thoughts. That was the confusing part about all of this. Fury slipped from my fingertips. I couldn't count the number of times the fire alarm went off at work this last month.

He would appear on the roof most nights, tapping the glass quietly, disrupting the little sleep I was managing. I'd climb out, and he'd whisk us away to his house. In his damn arms, everything faded away. He hung the moon and was well equipped to do so. The frenzy of our coupling only increased the intense emotions that poured from me. We spent a few seconds in each other's arms before he flashed me back to my bed. The unwanted grief at his leaving left me uncontrollable for hours. Unable to sleep, unable to do anything but stare at the faded ceiling. This wasn't healthy.

I sat on the stone bench, head in my hands. *Why did this have to be so confusing?* I did like him. We *could* sit for hours and talk, but there was something missing. If I could talk to Lyra, then maybe she would have an answer. *Hopefully.* If she ever answered her *goddamn* phone.

Gravel crunched in the distance signaling Kaity was almost here. We'd been meeting the last few weeks in the afternoon after my shifts. I mentioned to her when we started meeting that she could teleport to the range instead of driving, but she never did it in daylight. One of her mother's rules that Kaity still firmly believed in.

She came into the shelter area. One eyebrow raised as she asked, "No answer from your friend?"

While I had told her about not being able to get a hold of Lyra, I had yet to talk about what had gone down with Christo. Something held me back. Every time someone mentioned the cave or the rescued girls, it would be on the tip of my tongue, but I couldn't bring myself to utter the words.

"Ember?"

I looked at Kaity's expectant face. "Sorry. No, I haven't yet. It's not unusual."

"Hmm, seems weird with the technology available that she would be so far out of contact." Kaity sat down on the bench across from me.

I laughed. "Um yeah, she doesn't like technology. She has the one house in the only dead zone."

"Really?"

"Yeah. I've never been, but she seems to like to live off the grid."

We sat a few minutes longer. Kaity stared down at her phone screen while I checked mine again. *Should I try to visit Berkeley to see if Lyra was there?* Maybe Vanessa would have a wonderful insight into my madness. *A piece of ass? Joke's on me.*

"Ember?"

"Sorry, what did you say?"

"Do you want to get started?" she asked again, a ball of fire in her hand. "Are you okay? You've seemed off the last few weeks."

I nodded and followed her into the sand of the range. "I'm good. Ready for training."

We came out here four times a week to practice during the day together. Since I lost my bow in the caves, I needed to learn more combat techniques with my powers. While Kaity and I weren't exactly the same, we were close enough that she could help me with the fire. When I questioned whether it would really work or not, Kaity promised to only create fireballs so I had a fair chance.

I widened my stance and waited for fireballs to come hurtling toward me. As they got closer, I threw mine to deflect, sending them crashing into the sand near our feet. We went a few rounds before taking a break.

I was finally getting better. For the first few weeks, Kaity's hit me while I hadn't even landed one of mine close. I'd been more focused on creating them and not watching my surroundings. After our last round, we ventured to the benches to take a breather.

"Why do you wear that bracelet? Looks too bulky to be comfortable," Kaity asked, sitting down and grabbing her water bottle. She pointed to the cuff.

I tensed. *End of discussion.* The words rang in my mind.

Just breathe. "Not anymore. I've grown into it ever since Dad gave it to me when I was six." I rotated my arm to show Kaity the different clasps on the back. "He told me it belonged to my mother, and I wanted to be like her. And now it's just part of me."

"Wow, that's cool," Kaity said. Her hand reached for the pendant she wore around her neck. "My mother gave me this. Said Dad gave it to her as a wedding present."

The circular-shaped pendant held a diamond that glinted whenever the sun hit it.

"It's beautiful," I told her.

"Thank you." She jumped up and slammed her water down. "Let's get going."

"Do you know why Luke called a meeting at three?"

She shook her head. That made two of us. He texted earlier, before I left work at noon, and said to swing by the school for a special meeting. I half hoped it was about Hannah.

I climbed to my feet more slowly. "Anything on Hannah?" I asked for the third time that week.

She shook her head. "Nada, it's like she's vanished."

I clenched my fists. "Does that mean she's dead?"

Kaity tilted her head before she answered. "It could, or she's in a warded place where spells can't travel."

Passing the turnoff for home, I thought of Dad. We hadn't really talked in weeks. Both of us had been polite in the other's company since our disagreement. I'd hoped he would come around, but so far, nothing.

I followed Kaity to the school for the special meeting. We walked in together, and I noticed that there were a few more people than normal. Two young women, maybe around Kaity's age, sat at one of the tables talking to Luke and Ted. Nathan leaned against the bar with Grace as they laughed at one of Bob's jokes. We headed for Luke's table.

Luke watched as we approached. "Hey," he said, before he turned back to the two young women.

"Hey," Kaity and I said in unison.

Kaity giggled and sat beside one of the young women.

I didn't want to sit in between Kaity and Luke, so I walked around to sit beside Ted. I nodded to him as I swung my legs under the table. He lifted his head in greeting. He had come around since *the lecture*. Ted and Nathan both saw the work I put into patrolling and saving the women from the cave. Though Ted flinched the last time I lit a candle. *Big baby.*

"I'm glad you two are on time today," Luke said, and I rolled my eyes. *It was one time two weeks ago.* "Let me introduce you to our guests. They have some useful information."

I eyed Luke. What kind of useful information? My heart vibrated. *Hannah?* I waited for him, but one of the two girls spoke first.

She wore a navy-blue jean jacket. Her hair was twisted into a short ponytail. It appeared dark brown, but with the low lights, it could have been black. "I'm Sofia, and we heard your call about someone kidnapping young girls?"

The other girl continued, her hair dyed a pink color. "I'm Jasmine. A family friend of ours was kidnapped a few months ago." She sniffled, and I watched Sofia put a hand around her friend.

"We know who took her but can't find anyone that will help us."

"Why?" I questioned. "Can't you go to the police?"

Sofia's smile thinned. "The person who took her is the police around there. And after we talked to Luke here, we believe he's the same person who took your friend."

"How so?" Nathan asked. He and Grace walked over from the bar.

"He has preferences." She shivered.

And the air cooled around me. "You're a Zodian."

Sofia looked up at me. "Yes, we both are."

"Me too," I said, happy to meet more of my people.

They could have answers for me. *Everything I ever wanted to know.*

"Anyway," Sofia spoke again, "Jade has black hair, her skin is darker than ours. It's known that he is looking for someone."

"Who is he?" Luke questioned.

"Rabon," Jasmine whispered as if saying his name wasn't allowed.

"I've never heard of him," Ted said as he pulled his laptop out of the bag next to him.

"He's the king in San Fransico area, but his domain stretches across United States and beyond. He has several thousand vampires who follow him, along with a collection of demons."

"Who is he looking for? His demon henchman took almost ten women from around here," Kaity said from her seat at the table.

Sofia glanced at me. "You don't know?" she asked, and I shook my head. She pursed her lips. "From what the elders have gathered, he is searching for the Zodian Warrior."

"Zodian Warrior?" I asked, glancing at Luke. His eyes widened, and I knew he remembered the faraway night. When no one answered me, I looked back at Sofia who was staring at me. "I'm half Zodian. My dad is human, so I don't know about our culture." I gritted my teeth.

Jasmine reached her hand across the table to lay it upon mine. "Oh dear, that has to be hard."

"Anyway, what's the Zodian Warrior?"

"The legend is that the Zodian Warrior can control all elements and bring the Zodian back in order. Jade can wield both air and fire. Which is why he thinks she's the Zodian Warrior."

I sat back from the table. While I didn't know what that meant, I focused on the "all elements." "Doesn't every Zodian have the power to use all elements?"

Sofia gave me a look of sympathy. "Zodians can only use one. What's yours?"

"Ember controls fire," Grace chirped from her spot behind me.

Jasmine giggled. "The name suits you."

I smiled too. *It did suit me.*

"You think our missing girl is with your friend?" Luke asked. Sofia nodded. He continued, "A vampire dragged Hannah into a portal a month ago, and no one has seen her since. Kaity hasn't been able to locate her. What if she's not with your friend?"

Sofia sat straighter on the bench. "You help us rescue one person instead of two, and we thank you for that."

Luke sighed. He finally sat on the bench beside me. "What do we know of the location where she's being held?"

"I have someone else helping us," Sofia said, and we waited for her to continue. Her eyes darted across the room. "He's a demon but owes me a favor. He knows Rabon and is bringing us blueprints of the house and info on the comings and goings."

"That will be handy," Ted said, as he had spent the last few minutes trying to see if he could get a copy of the blueprints off the county website. "When will the blueprints be here?"

Sofia brought up her phone. "Soon. I told him where we were, and he said he knew of the place."

The door to the outside banged against the wall as someone strolled through.

Hell. What was *he* doing here? Heat pooled below; I squirmed in my seat, thankful all eyes were on Christo instead of me.

Cheer up, love. We'll have time for that later. It had taken several times for him speaking telepathically before it hadn't felt like an invasion inside my head.

He walked to the table and handed a roll of parchment to Sofia. It all clicked into place. He was *the demon. An Immortal Demon. An Immortal Demon Prince.* Funny, how I never pictured him as a demon even after we met and after everything that went down between us.

Better wipe that expression off your face.

I closed my mouth as I tried to listen to the surrounding conversation, but my mind wandered to the early morning sex. *Why hadn't he told me he was going to be here today?*

We spent the next few hours going over the details of Rabon's house. We made sure everyone knew where the watch would be, how many would be on guard, and where the exits were. Ted nudged me halfway through, and I made every effort to listen for the remainder of the time.

"What's this place here?" Ted asked Chris, pointing to what looked like a ballroom.

Christo decided to stand behind me, off to the side. His presence overwhelmed me, and I wondered if anyone would think it odd for me to escape to the bathroom. As he talked, he moved over closer to Sofia, giving me much-needed space.

Chris nodded. "It's a foyer, but it's the only place in the house where someone can teleport in or out. He's sealed the house with protection spells."

We went through the plans again, double-checking they were all solid.

Chris stood beside Sofia, in the perfect spot for me to observe his facial expressions. He seemed at ease in the room even as my heart raced. *What if they find out?* Chris cocked his body to the side and smiled in my direction before he addressed the room.

"There's one small catch."

"Catch?" Sofia and Luke said together.

Chris's smile faded. "My sources say that the only time he will be gone from the house in the next week will be in two days and only for two hours between three and five in the morning."

Luke shifted beside me, grazing my thigh under the table, and the link between Chris and me tightened. I coughed. Luke patted me on the back harder than necessary, which made me cough worse. He gave me a pointed stare, and I nodded.

Luke glanced at the plans on the table. "Here's my plan. It's pretty straightforward. At three fifteen, we leave here. We'll observe the house before we teleport inside. Once inside, the two teams will search each of the two floors in the house. We meet back in one hour in the foyer, even if we don't find them. Is that agreed?" He eyed Sofia and Jasmine. They both nodded slowly. "Then we're ready," Luke said as he picked up his phone. "We've been at it for several hours. Let's meet back here tomorrow at midnight to discuss any final plans."

Everyone agreed. Sofia and Jasmine walked out.

"Hey, do you guys have a place to stay?" Kaity yelled when they made it to the door.

"No, not yet."

Do you want me to take you home?

I stiffened in my seat as I glanced over at Christo, standing tall with a smug-ass grin on his face.

I'll be fine. I drove here all on my own. I shot back through our connection, then refocused on the other Zodians who were chatting with Kaity.

"You can stay with me. I have plenty of room," Kaity suggested.

Bye, love. See you tonight.

They all disappeared before I could respond. *Damnit, why can't I ever get my answers?*

"Ember."

I glanced behind me to see that Luke and I were the only ones left.

"Yeah," I said as I stood from the table.

"Are you all right?" He headed to the bar, returning with a clear liquor bottle and two glasses. He poured drinks. "You seemed off tonight. Your heart was beating a mile a minute. Are you worried about going with that demon?"

To bed? Nah, I got that covered. Heat flushed my cheeks. "Um, no, I'm good." I downed the shot, coughing at the burn of the vodka. *Not my favorite.*

"You're sure?"

I nodded before leaving the school. The intense emotions around Christo had stopped when he left. He'd mentioned in passing that we were in the honeymoon phase. *When will this shit end?* I laughed, then hiccupped as I climbed into my car.

Twenty-four

EMBER

The time clock beeped as I swiped the badge, grateful the end of the day had finally arrived. I checked my phone for the third time. Kaity had yet to respond to whether she would have time for a session today with our other plans tonight.

The midafternoon sun beat down as I drove through downtown Happy Valley, but as I neared the turnoff for the main road out of town, I decided to swing by Kaity's house first. Hopefully, the two new Zodians would be there.

I shut off the car in Kaity's driveway, taken aback by the old Victorian house. I'd never been here though she'd invited me for dinner on several occasions. The white paint was chipped on every panel. Green moss grew on one side of the house, and tall weeds surrounded the lower half. The walkway leading to the front porch was cracked, allowing the grass to grow in between.

I stepped carefully onto the stairs, missing the half-broken plank as I ascended to the porch. The paint on the front door, once a vibrant yellow, was now faded and weathered. The oval glass inlay was cracked from one side to the other.

The door swung open before I could knock. Kaity stood there dressed in shorts and a green sleeveless top. Her hair was half pulled into a messy bun.

"Hey," Kaity said, waving her hand for me to enter.

I walked into the entrance and stopped to admire the old grandfather clock. I listened to the seconds tick by as the pendulum swung back and forth.

"What's up?" Kaity asked beside me.

Before I could speak, laughter came from another part of the house. I turned in that direction.

"Did you want to speak with Jasmine and Sofia? They plan to stay with me until we finish this business with that monster Rabon." Kaity headed down the hallway and continued to chatter. "They've told me hellacious stories of him and his brother. They dislike your people."

"Oh," I murmured, glancing at the artwork on the walls we passed in the hallway.

Kaity stopped and turned back to me. "Yeah, I guess you probably don't know any of that since you weren't raised like them."

Another reminder that I didn't know who I was. Didn't think it would come from her, and I knew deep down she didn't mean it hurtfully. I nodded my head as we continued into the back of the house.

A kitchen was off to the right and a living room on

the left. The two Zodians sat on a loveseat before a fireplace where ash rested at the bottom.

We exchanged hellos as I sat down with Kaity. The couch was decorated with a bright array of yellow and blue flowers. The tattered cushions gave way to my weight, and I found myself closer to the ground than I thought I would be.

"Ember, it's good to see you again," Sofia said, lounging on the opposite couch identical to the one I sat on. She turned to Jasmine. "We were telling Kaity about the start of the conflict between the Zodian and the Chaos Brothers."

"Chaos Brothers?" I asked.

She nodded. "Yep, the name sounds silly, but it makes grown men wet themselves."

I leaned forward. "They're that bad? Who are they?"

Jasmine piped in, "Istros and Rabon."

"And they are?"

"Creatures created by the God Zamolxis. He created the horrible Kogani wolves, too."

Wolves? I thought they were talking about brothers, but before I could ask about the wolves, Sofia continued on.

"Zamolxis created the brothers to serve him by creating chaos in the world. The chaos strengthens his powers."

"That sounds ridiculous. Gods don't exist," Kaity chimed in and caught my eye. I silently agreed with her. "Why does chaos strengthen him?"

Both girls turned to face each other, an unsure look on their faces.

"You don't know?" I asked and crossed my legs as I tried to find a comfortable position, but I sank further into the couch.

Sofia shrugged her shoulders. "Well, no. They were created centuries ago. "

"That's good to know." I rolled my eyes and made Kaity giggle beside me.

"Do you want to know?" Jasmine snapped at me.

"Sorry," I said. "Please continue."

"Now, where was I?" Sofia spoke again. "The Chaos Brothers were created before our people became Zodians. They terrorized the regions north of where our tribes were located, not bothering us until after invaders from the south tried to wipe us out. The God Zodi bestowed the gifts of the elements upon us. Once we defeated the invaders, the Chaos Brothers recognized us as a source of power. The first Great Circle happened to determine the new leader of the tribes. That's when we became the Zodian."

I turned to look at Sofia. "Who won?"

She gave me a pointed look.

I clenched my fists at my side. When Jasmine's attention slid down, I tucked my hands under my knees as Sofia explained that the thirteenth tribe had been victorious in that first circle.

"Has there been more than one?" I asked.

Sofia nodded. "There's been two in our history."

"Who won the last one?" Kaity asked.

I half nodded at her, relieved she'd asked for me.

Sofia leaned forward. "The thirteenth tribe won both Great Circles, but after the second one happened, the thirteenth tribe scattered. Our people weren't sure they had survived the attack from the Chaos Brothers."

Christo's recitation of my people's history repeated in my head.

"Why did the Chaos Brothers attack?"

Jasmine resumed the story. "A daughter was born to the reigning king and queen, but a seer foresaw she would destroy the Chaos Brothers."

Sofia smiled. "This is where it gets good."

I didn't share her enthusiasm. It sounded more like the end of the Zodians.

"When the king and queen heard the prophecy, they sent their daughter into hiding. They kept her hidden for eighteen years, but at a celebration in honor of their daughter's marriage, the Chaos Brothers attacked. They killed an entire city full of Zodians, humans, and other supernaturals. It's been named the Fall of the Heavens as the king and queen died in order for their daughter to escape."

"But she didn't escape," Kaity said beside me in a low tone.

I smiled her way before I focused on the other Zodians. Neither one of them had noticed our exchange.

"The princess fought Rabon. We don't know what exactly happened, but Rabon fell and so did the princess. Istros was the only one to walk out of Heaven Hall."

Something didn't add up. "If she killed Rabon, how is he alive today?"

They exchanged looks. "He's immortal. If he or his brother dies, they will be reborn."

I leaned back. "Is there a way to kill him?"

Sofia shrugged. "None that the council of twelve have found."

Council of twelve? Who were they? But more importantly. "How do we kill him now?"

"Oh, we won't. The goal is to retrieve our friends," Jasmine said. Her face deflated, she moved her arm, and a mark caught my eye.

"You have a mark?" I rushed, excitement filling me. My fingers touched my bracelet.

Jasmine glanced down at her mark. "Yeah, so should you . . ." Her face deflated. "But you didn't live in a tribe."

"What does that have to do with the mark?"

Sofia's eyes softened. "It's part of the rite of passage." She pulled her sleeve up to show a mark that looked like the little dipper. "When we turn eight, the Shaman holds a ceremony to celebrate the element that chooses you. Water chose me to wield it."

"It's a grand party, but you didn't have one, so your mark wouldn't have been established like ours," Jasmine said. She traced her finger around the triangle that had a sideways hockey stick across the top. "Air chose me."

"Oh, I see," I said, bringing my hand down. *How did I get my mark then?* "And that's the only way?" They both nodded. "So, what tribe do you guys belong to?" I asked.

Jasmine and Sofia exchanged glances. "We're in the ninth tribe, Orra."

"I wonder what my tribe is?"

Jasmine shook her head. "Hm, I don't know. Didn't your mother ever tell you?"

I tensed at her words. "My mother died when I was very young, and my father being human, didn't know how to get in contact with anyone," I explained. "Is there a book on the different tribes?"

"Nah," Jasmine said. "With Rabon killing us off, each tribe sticks together, and only shamans track our histories."

"Shamans hold meetings with the other tribes each year, but only certain members are allowed."

I sat back against the couch, sinking into the cushions as if it were hugging me. Christo's explanation was the most I'd gotten. I had really hoped these two would confirm what he said.

Kaity broke the tension as she headed into the kitchen. She called over her shoulder. "How do we get into Rabon's house, fight him, and save our friends?"

"The demon," Sofia started.

"You mean Chris," I said and inwardly regretted the words.

"His name is Chris, but I like to call him *demon* to remind myself that he is, in fact, a demon who could kill me."

I nodded and looked at my jeans to pick at the invisible speck of lint. "I should go."

"Did you want me to come out with you?" Kaity asked.

"Where?" Jasmine asked.

And before I could say anything to deter them, Kaity responded with how she's been helping me with training.

"Oh, I love to get a workout in." Sofia jumped off the couch. "Can we come?"

"Sure, why not?" I doubted I would have to fight one of my own kind in the future, but it wouldn't be bad to learn how to defend myself from similar powers. I headed out with the reassurance that they would meet me in thirty minutes. That would give me time to call Lyra again.

Twenty-five

EMBER

The drive seemed shorter than normal, but my mind repeated the information I'd received. I walked to the covered concrete and slid my phone out. Once Lyra's number appeared on the screen again, I pushed send. This was the longest she'd ghosted me, and part of me wondered if she was in trouble.

"Hello," a voice came through.

I paused and opened my mouth to spit out my normal *Call me back, please* phrase before I realized she had answered the call.

"Lyra?" I asked.

"No shit, Sherlock," said Lyra. "You called me."

I smiled at her snarky attitude. "Sorry, it's been a while since you answered. We missed several sessions." I heard her sigh through the phone speaker. "Do you not want to help me anymore?" Did I finally get on her nerves enough that she wanted to cut me out?

Silence followed until I heard a voice in the background. "Look, kid, it's not that. I have a day job, and I've been busy."

She paused. I could just make out what the other person said. "Where should we dump the body?"

What?

"I need to go, but I know your messages sounded urgent. I'll call you back later tonight, okay?"

I nodded. "Of course." The phone went dead.

I pulled it from my ear, and I glanced around as the aether alerted me that Kaity, Jasmine, and Sofia were arriving. Kaity, despite her rules, had used magic to teleport them to the range. Their faces were upturned as if they had been laughing moments before.

Kaity stepped forward. "Are you all right? You left so fast I didn't get a chance to say we could have all teleported together."

I nodded. "That's okay. I plan to stay here to practice."

Kaity nodded as she returned to the other two girls.

"What do you use this place for?" Jasmine asked as she eyed the deserted area.

"It's a gun range owned by the county." I put my phone face down on one of the tables.

"What do you want to learn?" Sofia came to stand beside me.

"Um, well, Kaity has been helping me learn how to fight with my powers. I haven't had any formal training."

Jasmine squealed, "We can take turns sparring," before she walked out onto the sand. "Let's begin."

I stepped off the concrete to face her. "Ready?"

She smiled, but the air stirred beside her lifting small pebbles of sand an inch from the ground. A windstorm slammed into me, knocking me back several feet.

I clenched my fist and took a step back to balance myself. I closed my eyes as the aether filtered in and out. While it kept me informed on Jasmine's whereabouts, I imagined a wall of fire to block off the wind.

"Wow," someone said.

I opened my eyes, surprised by a wall of fire that stood seven feet tall, big enough to block Jasmine's storm from all sides. Jasmine's smile tightened into a grimace, and she waved her hands in an arc as I sensed the wind shift to the side.

With my hand relaxed, I took a deep breath as the wall of fire moved closer and closer to Jasmine. Finally, as I exhaled, the wall surrounded her, cutting off the wind.

"Ember wins!" Kaity yelled, and I let the fire go.

Jasmine stomped off the range to lean against the pavilion post.

"Sorry," I yelled to her. I didn't mean to scare her.

"You won't beat me that fast," Sofia called from the spot Jasmine had left.

Before I half turned, a stream of water hit me in the shoulder, knocking me off balance. My hands scraped against the hard ground as I landed. Hair on my arms tingled, and I rolled out of the way, dodging the next stream.

I stood; water dripped onto the ground. I clenched my fist as heat radiated out of me, drying my clothes instantly. *Damn, I didn't know I could do that.* I scanned Sofia and let a smile play on my lips. *I could do this.*

Sofia geared for another attack, waving her hands in a circle above her head. The air buzzed with electricity the moment she attacked. *I got you.* Now, I knew what to sense. I would be ready for her next attack.

Concentrating on making my firewall again, I took a deep breath. Air stirred in front of me. I called forth the fire. I could see it building in my mind.

I blocked the water aimed at me. Steam rose as the fire hit the water. I took a step forward and pushed the wall closer to Sofia.

It looked like she was losing as I took steps closer. Her water sizzled against the fire. I listened to the aether but wasn't fast enough to block the water that hit me from the side.

The fire disappeared as water drenched me from head to foot. I swayed from the push of the water, trying to keep my balance. I barely had time to take a last breath before being submerged. As the water flowed around my body, I watched in horror as the ground got farther and farther away.

I tried to claw out of my prison as blurry figures moved around me. One was inches from me. Sofia. If I panicked, I could *die.* Closing my eyes and releasing the tension from my body, I visualized the outcome I wanted. I knew, at any moment, I would need to take a breath of air. I called forth fire. If I could light my entire body like in the cave, I could boil the water into steam. *Hopefully.*

Panic flooded me as my fire wouldn't light. To keep

from breathing, I raised my hand to cover my mouth. Blackness crept from the sides of my vision.

"Ember," I heard Kaity's voice through the water.

I dropped onto the hard ground again. I rolled to my back, gasping for air, and immediately rolled back over to cough up water.

"Ember," Kaity yelled, reaching my side. "Are you okay?" She patted my back as I coughed.

"Yeah," I breathed, taking in a long drag of fresh air.

A shadow fell over my face. Sofia. Through blurry vision, I saw a sneer on her face, but then concern appeared as it cleared.

"Oh my gosh, I'm sorry. I don't know my strength sometimes," she said as she bent to help me stand.

I coughed before I could answer her. "Yeah, I'm fine." Although, I wasn't completely sure as my lungs burned.

"I'm sorry, Ember," she repeated before she backed away to stand with Jasmine.

Kaity turned my face in her direction gently. "Are you okay?"

I nodded, talking hurt. She stepped back. As my body swayed, I clenched my hands before balancing myself. I ventured into the pavilion, sitting down at a table as I watched Kaity and Sofia take a round. The match seemed even, but in the end, Sofia won like she had against me. Instead of encompassing Kaity in water, she made octopus arms and knocked Kaity to the sand. She pointed an ice pick at her neck until Kaity conceded. That had been an intense moment, and I stood, fist engulfed in flames, ready to help Kaity if Sofia went too far. Was her intent to kill me? *Could we trust them?*

Next, Jasmine and Sofia did a round. This one didn't last long as Sofia wiped the floor with Jasmine.

"Well, we better go." Jasmine looked toward the sky. "It's getting late."

The purple sky told me we'd been out here for a couple of hours. I would need to head home for dinner soon.

"See you tonight."

The three of them joined hands before they disappeared.

I sat down next to my phone to text Dad I would be late for supper. I needed a minute.

Was Sofia trying to kill me? Why would she? I'd never met her before last night. Did my questions earlier annoy her that much?

With head in hands, I sighed. Sofia trying to kill me sounded crazy, but what else was that? She knew I knew little about my powers in a fight. The firewall enclosed Jasmine, but Sofia hadn't known it was the first time I'd done it intentionally.

The phone beside me started ringing. I lifted my head to answer. Lyra? I pushed the talk button and speaker.

"Hello?"

"Sorry about earlier, kid." Lyra's voice came through clearer. "What did you need?"

I wanted to talk about Christo, but now with Sofia's

attack fresh in my mind, I needed to know how to avoid that.

"I hope you have time to talk because I . . ." My voice trailed off as lightning flashed in the distance.

"Yes, all night. What's going on?"

"Can a Zodian travel through a storm?"

"Travel?" repeated Lyra. "What do you mean?"

"I got into some trouble."

"Let's hear it?"

Surprise flickered through me at the concern in Lyra's voice. I knew she cared about me, but she'd always been a sarcastic type of person. None came through now.

"The others and I were tracking the missing girls. We found the vampires who had been taking them. They're working for a demon. We fought in a cave under Happy Valley." I paused and took a breath. This was harder than I thought it would be to tell her all of it. I was such an idiot.

"Go on."

"I used my bow to take out some vampires, but then I fought the demon. He was stronger than me." The demon's red eyes flashed before me. Shivering, I wrapped my arms around myself. "He had me pinned, but I guess my powers kicked in, and I engulfed us in flames."

"You're not hurt, are you?" Lyra asked. "Do you need me to jump on a plane?"

While Lyra was flaky half the time, she did care. "No, I'm fine, I think."

"You think?" she asked.

"After the flames engulfed me, I passed out and woke

up in a stranger's house." I took another deep breath. "Not a stranger. I met him at Berkeley during a semester, but he wasn't a friend."

"Who?"

"His name is Christo." I heard Lyra's indrawn breath through the speaker. *Did she know him?*

"What happened?" she said in a harsh voice.

"Everything seemed fine at first. He had called a healer for my injury. Apparently, the demon had pulled a knife out and stabbed me before I could burn him alive. I didn't realize he actually hit me."

"What happened? You're skirting around the actual issue. Tell me."

"I stayed with him, and on the last afternoon, I slept with him. It's not something I normally do, but I'm drawn to him for some reason," I rambled. "When I woke, everything was weird."

"Weird how?"

"He kept hearing my thoughts." I paused again. *Would she believe me?* This sounded crazy now, even a month later. "He explained it was part of their culture. That we were now bonded."

"He bonded with you?" Lyra spat; a loud noise followed. *Did she knock something over?*

"Yes, that's what he said. We argued, and I ran. When I realized I didn't know how to get home and he was chasing me, I wanted to be safe and away from him. The next thing I knew, I stood in the middle of a road in Happy Valley."

Silence followed the end of my story. If Lyra was

processing, I couldn't tell. The only sound came from the crickets around me.

"Is it possible to travel?"

"Is that what you're concerned about?" she questioned.

I shook my head. "No, but it's probably an easier answer than whether I can be unbonded from a demon."

"Yes, the short answer is yes. Powerful Zodians can do it. My mother used it in battle."

Lyra was a Zodian. I knew it.

"Ember," Lyra yelled

I turned to the phone. "Yes, I'm here."

She tsked. "I don't know a way to break the bond except for death."

My hands clenched. I knew that would be her answer. "I don't know what I'm doing. Maybe I should open the box. It would be so much easier."

I wiped the wetness from my cheeks as the approaching storm crackled in the distance.

"Who would you be?" Lyra asked. "And while being bonded isn't ideal, it's not a complete loss. He can't lie to you or you'll know through the bond, but it changes your life outlook. And besides, giving your powers away won't undo the bond."

My fingers combed through my hair as I considered what she was telling me. He couldn't lie, and that would be handy. "I don't want to be tied to anyone. I'm trying to figure out who I am."

"I know some people within the Immortal Society. I'll

ask around. See if there is another way. Until then, play along. The Immortals are a patriarchal society."

"Like I need this complication. I can't get Dad to talk about my mother."

"I know." She paused. "Don't stop now. You can do this. Traveling through lightning like you did means you're getting better."

"I doubt that."

"Why?" she asked.

"Some Zodians came into town yesterday, and today we practiced together. One of them used air, and I built a wall of fire to surround her. But her friend controlled water. She encased me. Tried to drown me. I don't know if she meant it or not."

"Who was she?"

"Her name is Sofia, that's all I know." I leaned against the table to stretch my back. "They came to town looking for some help with their missing friend."

"How can you help?"

"It turns out Hannah and their friend could be kept at the same location. We're planning a rescue tomorrow."

"Be careful."

"I will, and the fondant on the cake is that Christo is helping. So, I'll have to hide my relationship with him from the others."

"That's not the saying," laughed Lyra. "Why are you hiding it?"

I shrugged my shoulders. "Why should I tell my friends how royally I screwed up? I was hoping you would have a solution."

"Keeping all these secrets isn't good for you, kid," said Lyra.

She was probably right, but I couldn't help it. Between Dad, Luke, and the others, I had a secret with everyone in my life. While I think we cleared any romantic issues between us, I knew Luke would try to help me with Christo. And every time I thought about telling him, the reaction in my head made me cringe. He would want to help solve my problem. Right now, the only way to do that was to kill Christo. And I wasn't entirely sure who would win. *Or if I wanted Christo dead.*

I turned the conversation back to Sofia. "Lyra, what can I do to keep from being drowned?"

"You've realized by now that you have control over more than one element."

"Yes, of course." We realized that at one of my first sessions.

"That's the solution."

"What?"

"You can control the water as you control fire and air. Take control of the situation."

That made sense. "If people know I can control more than one element, what does that mean?" Did that mean I was the Zodian Warrior?

"It means you're special, and you have always been special."

"Sofia said the Zodian Warrior could control all the elements. Can I do that?"

A door slammed through the phone. "I've gotta go,

kid."

The line went dead. Why couldn't people answer simple questions? Why were they all keeping so many secrets buried? *Dad. Lyra.*

Twenty-six

EMBER

Two hours late for dinner, I walked into an empty kitchen. Dad and I had been silently living together this past month. He still cooked meals, and I ate them. The counters were clean—no dirty pan sat in the sink or leftovers on the stove. No faint smell of food.

We were polite to each other, which was normal for us, but deep down, I knew the argument had broken something. Dad would hardly look at me during dinner. Never asked questions about the bank anymore. An emptiness filled me whenever I was at home, which was one reason I spent most of last month at Parker Elementary. Dad hardly asked where I went, but the need to tell him was ingrained in me. I'd text him that I was with Grace, even though most of the time, I sat in an empty cafeteria with Luke drinking Bob's outrageous concoctions.

A noise from the hallway grabbed my attention.

"Dad?" I asked, as he tugged at a suitcase stuck in the closet. "What are you doing?"

"Hey," he huffed.

"Hey." I pointed at the suitcase.

"Last-minute conference. I need to go to Berkeley."

I moved a box of targets to free the suitcase. "Will it at least be an interesting topic?"

He leaned and stretched out his back. "I doubt it. Some new tax law going into effect next year we need to be prepared for."

I held the closet door shut while Dad bolted the lock. We smiled as I pulled the suitcase into the dining room. The first warmth from him in weeks spread through me.

"I'll be gone for three days," he said. "Will you be all right alone here while I'm gone?"

"Of course. I'll probably stay with Grace tomorrow?"

"That's not a problem. I'll be back late on the third night. No need to wait on me."

"When do you leave?"

"First light. Flight leaves around nine. Conference starts at two o'clock." He picked up the suitcase and headed to his room. "Good night. Food's in the fridge if you're hungry."

⊷─────⊶

I awoke to the sound of Dad's SUV leaving at the crack of dawn. I stood in front of his door. I turned to look behind me. No one was there. *Was this a bad idea? Breaking into Dad's locked room?*

I nodded. "I have to do this," I whispered.

While not the best idea I've had, it needed to be done. With the distance that had grown between us these last couple of weeks, I'd stopped asking questions about Mom.

I jiggled the knob. *Locked as always.* I bent down in front of the keyhole, pulling an old bobby pin from my pocket that I'd found in the bathroom. I pushed it into the hole and gave it a hard twist. Something clicked, then the twisted wire rebounded and snapped straight out of my fingers. It slipped through the hole and landed on the other side of the door. *Damn. Fuck.* I hit my forehead against the door, and it squeaked open.

His room was a decent size, bare of all emotion. Just a bed against one wall, a nightstand, and a dresser. The top of the dresser held the single sentimental picture of Dad's parents. Dad resembled his mother. I plucked the frame from its perch. It had been taken when Dad was a toddler before his older sister had been killed. She looked to be around ten. I knew nothing else about her. He never discussed his family. His parents had come a few times over the years but mostly stayed away, which I had always been grateful for since Grandma Sue had a perpetual sneer for me. I put the picture back down and looked around the room once more.

Now, if I were a key, where would I be? Better yet, if I were Dad and wanted to hide something from his only daughter, where would I put it?

I opened the bedside table first and combed through old receipts, the black licorice wrappers, spare change, and headphones tied in a knot. I took everything out and laid it out on top of the table, then placed my hand inside the drawer to make sure I missed nothing. *Empty.* I slid everything back into the drawer, shutting it.

Now where? I eyed the dresser but wasn't ready to go through my dad's undies. I crossed to the closet. He had his dress clothes for work on one side, workout clothes on the other side, and his polos and khakis in the middle. I moved some shirts to see the back of the closet. *Nada.*

I moved the clothes back the other way to see the other side of the closet. There was nothing but a quarter-shaped hole. I leaned in closer. It was smooth and worn from use. I put my finger into the hole and pulled. The panel shifted. *A hidden compartment?* I yanked the board off and moved it aside. A leather accordion bag sat inside. I placed it on the carpet in front of me. Slowly, I opened the lid and sifted through the papers. Tax returns were filed in the first few spots, but my name on a label jumped out at me.

Emma Ellington.

I pulled the documents out of the slot and read over my birth certificate. Nothing looked out of place. Born January first at midnight. Makani Ellington was listed as my mother but no maiden name. I put the certificate back in the box and looked down at the next paper.

What the hell? I pulled the other paper out and laid them side by side.

Why would there be two separate filings? Both were birth certificates, but they weren't the same.

On one, Emma Ellington was typed under "name"

and Makani Ellington under my mother's. On the second document, those names read as Ember Storm and Makani Storm. Heath Ellington was only listed as the father on the first document.

I scanned the rest of the documents, but nothing stood out. I found the deed to the house, all of the life insurance policies, and health records. My school records and dental records, but the one thing missing was Dad's connection to my mom.

A leaf blower sounded outside, making me jump and drop the papers. *Good grief.* This was ridiculous. Was my mother's maiden name Storm? But what reason would he have to hide that fact from me? Or even on the certificates themselves? I'd never thought to ask Gran Serafina when she'd been around. Why did he have two birth certificates for me but no marriage license or death certificate for my mother? None of this was making sense.

I stuffed everything back in the leather satchel, hiding it back behind the panel again before sitting on my knees to look in the bottom of the closet for my prize. I sifted through his shoes. As I stood, the sunshine shining into the room glinted off something silver, catching my eye.

I pulled out an old wood box with silver corners. It was maybe the size of a jewelry box. I turned it around in my hands, not finding a latch. I wiped the top of the box. The dust made me cough. I immediately noticed the symbol. *The mark.* Interconnected golden triangles were inlaid on the top of the box.

"This was my mother's."

I sat there on the floor of Dad's closet for a few more minutes as I tried to open the wood box but had no luck. The real prize was still hidden. I'd come to find a key, though this box was an awesome bonus. The key had to be somewhere. My eyes landed on the dresser. The last place to check.

I crossed to the dresser and started at the bottom, then worked my way up. I took a deep breath. The first couple of drawers were plain. Old workout clothes, some college T-shirts neatly folded. The third drawer, middle drawer, housed old photos of Dad's younger days with family and friends.

I didn't recognize anyone in the photos except for his family. But, under it all, this drawer held a cigar box. My heart beat faster.

I retrieved the box and sat on the bed. I lifted the lid slowly, hoping nothing too private was inside. The box contained various receipts, several showing a rebate that was long since overdue. I shifted my position sideways on the bed and dumped the contents. Then I pulled out all the receipts and placed them to the side. Next, jewelry laid in a tangle. I combed through the silver but still didn't see the key.

I took a deep breath, closing my eyes as my vision started to blur. *That's it.* My fingers wrapped around the edge of the wood box, flinging it away from me. It crashed into the wall, making a tiny divot in the plaster. *Fuck.* I picked the box up, thankful that it hadn't broken, the lid was a little loose, but it would do. I turned the box over, seeing that the inside velvet pad detached from the bottom. As I walked, a rattling noise came from inside. I lifted the pad out, and there sat a shiny silver key. *Is this it?*

I removed the tiny key, left the mess on the bed, and rushed out to the hall closet to check. The key slid into the slot. I couldn't hold back my grin as I turned it in the lock. *Click.* I pulled the door open, and the aether vibrated around me. The long wooden box was almost identical to the one in Dad's closet, confirming my suspicion that both belonged to my mother. I pulled it out of the cabinet, sitting it on the floor in front of me. This box had a latch unlike the other. I wasted no time in opening the lid to gaze down at my mother's sword.

Dad's story never did its beauty justice.

I lifted the blade and pulled it out of its sheath, eyeing the beauty. It wasn't very long, more like a short sword. The pommel held a bloodstone that continued down the sides of the handle in between the darkened leather. The blade was linked down the center, and the steel was etched to resemble the four elements. I laid it in my hand, trying to find the slit where it became two swords. The slight touch against the edge sliced my finger. Blood dropped onto the blade. Letters shimmered in the light, seemingly woken by my touch. I squinted down at the word. *Warrior. Zodian Warrior?*

I sheathed the blade and laid it beside me, and searched the fur lining for anything else. I closed the box and replaced it exactly as it had been before in the closet. I locked the door and went back to stash the key where I'd found it.

Once I made sure everything was back in its original place, I locked and closed the door behind me. I carried the wood box and sword to my room.

On my way through the living room, the clock told me I was already running late. I still needed to pack for my girl's night with Grace and the raid. With my backpack full of my clothes, my mother's box, and the sword wrapped in a blanket, I ran out and down the steps. I loaded the car with my supplies, then sped to work, yawning.

My day was plagued with concerns about the rescue attempt ahead of us. Luke had chosen me to go with Sofia and Christo. While we didn't know if we could trust Sofia, Christo was another matter entirely. Despite how our relationship started, I knew he couldn't lie to me. He seemed to care for me even though he barely knew me.

Twenty-seven

EMBER

I climbed out of the car and watched Grace bolt down her stairs, waving. I grabbed my bag from the front seat.

"Hey," I yelled across the yard.

Grace trotted over to me, barely stopping herself from barreling into me. "It's been forever."

I dropped my bag on the ground and hugged her back. "I know." My voice was muffled through her hair and sweater. I pulled away from her. "I've got something to show you." I steered her around to the trunk that I had popped open when I parked. I threw the blanket off. My mother's sword lay there in the trunk in all its glory.

"What is that?" she asked as her hands inched toward it. "A sword? Where did you get it?"

Picking it up, I smiled. "It was my mother's."

Grace watched as I unsheathed the blade. "It's beautiful."

"It's two short swords."

"How?"

I handed the blade to her. "Not sure yet. But be careful, it's super sharp."

Grace swung the sword around a few feet from me.

"How did you get it?" asked Grace.

I shifted and displaced the gravel under my feet. "I saw it once when I was a girl. Dad was holding it in our hallway late at night with tears streaming down his face, but I stayed in the shadows, watching how delicately he handled it. The blade sparkled in the hall light. It was like it called to me. I desperately wanted to hold it, but I slipped on the stairs. Dad put the box back in the locked cabinet. I guess I just let myself forget it was there. A few nights ago, he had it out, and I saw it. I knew I needed to have it. It's part of my history."

I looked up to find Grace crying. She wiped a few tears. "I'm sorry your dad's such an ass. I can't comprehend why he is so unwilling to talk to you about your own mother."

Silent, I watched the tears spill down her face. It seemed out of place that she was more upset. I was the one dealing with it. I shrugged my shoulders. "It hurts him too much to talk about her."

A cough-like laugh came out of Grace. "Sorry. It's no excuse. He's hurting you more and needs therapy. The more he remembers your mother, the less it would hurt over time, and he would have made fresh memories with you." Grace twirled the sword one last time before handing it back to me. "Anyway, it's super lightweight. Bring it. Let's go to the backyard."

"Are your parents home?" I asked, sheathing the blade and collecting my discarded backpack as I followed Grace into her backyard.

"No, they went to my grandmother's and won't be back until tomorrow."

"That's nice. Dad is off at a conference and won't be back either. We don't have to worry about them finding out what we have planned tonight."

The faint sounds of bugs stirred to life with the end of the day. I sat my bag at the edge of the patio and followed Grace to where a fire pit sat beside the pond. I enjoyed the moment. The sun dipped into the background. A nice pinkish and purple sky stretched out above us.

I leaned the sword against one of the folding chairs that sat around the fire pit. "Why did we come out here? I'm starving. Weren't we ordering pizza?"

"Um, well, can you help me?" Grace asked.

Her focus was on the pond instead of me. I crossed to stand beside her. "Help with what?"

She sighed with her arms. *Dramatic*, the word Dad used to describe Grace.

"My mentor has been trying for months to teach me how to shoot beams of light out of my hand, but it never works. Maybe since you can control fire, you could help."

"I guess they're similar," I said. "What has the mentor taught you?"

Grace took a few steps back from me and took a pose.

Her legs shoulder width apart. Her eyes closed, and her mouth moved like she counted down. Finally, she held out her right palm, face up toward the fire pit. I waited, but nothing happened.

"See," she whined, planting her face in her hands.

"No, what were you doing?" I asked, walking to stand beside her, more out of the path. "Would it help if you imagined the burn pile as someone you dislike?" Grace whipped her head up. "I mean, have you forgiven Missy from that time in grade school?"

Grace put her hand up. "We are not talking about that time. Forgotten but never forgiven. Besides, my mentor said I shouldn't have hateful thoughts when using my powers. They gave my powers with love, and I should only use that. But that hasn't worked yet."

"Love," I repeated. "Think about it this way. If a vampire was draining your mother dry, and you were the only one that could save her. Focus on the love you have for the people you want to help."

Before our eyes, a beam of light shot out, missed the burn pile, and hit one of the folding chairs, knocking it over with a giant hole burned through the back of it.

At the same time, I jumped back from Grace, landed on a stick, and my feet rolled out from under me. I landed on my ass, watching the beam hit the pond and dissipate.

"Are you okay?" Grace held her hands out to help me up.

I climbed to my feet, brushing off the dead leaves. I smirked. "See, you're getting it now."

Grace rolled her eyes as she returned to the same spot to try again.

I watched Grace process her feelings, but eventually, after several more attempts, the burn pile lit up.

"Good job," I said as I walked over to sit the folding chair back into position, hoping her parents didn't ask about the hole.

"Thanks for helping. My mentor will be super impressed next week at our session!"

I nodded as she smiled my way.

"It feels good to take a break from everything tonight. I was with the Collective all afternoon telling them about our plans." Grace turned to head back to the house. "Let's go watch some *Gossip Girl* reruns."

"Wait, why would they care about the mission tonight?"

She turned back toward me. "I'm Luke's champion. There's some kind of prophecy that he's going to save the world. It's my job to make sure he stays alive until he can fulfill his role."

I kept my focus on Grace's face as she spoke. This wasn't nonsense to her. "Is that why you check on him during the day?"

Her eyes widened at my question. "Yeah. Let's go watch some drama. I snagged a bottle of Bob's latest margarita concoction." She pointed at me and then slowly turned her wrist, motioning with her finger to follow her. "You are *not* making me drink by myself."

I smiled and agreed to one drink. We needed to be sober for the mission later.

I stayed in my spot as Grace got closer to the house, thinking about what she said. She really did believe there was a prophecy out there about Luke. The only prophecy I'd heard of was the Zodian Warrior from Sofia and Jasmine. While they seemed okay, there was something there that had me wary. I had gotten a faint whiff of death, nothing like vampires or even Christo. It seemed puzzling. Why did death cling to them? *Could they also sense the aether?*

While I knew how the aether worked, I sometimes wondered if it could be wrong. Bob's signature reminded me of old sitcoms, while Luke's brought forth feelings of freedom, and Christo's was like the fumes of black licorice. I shuddered at the memory of Dad's favorite candy.

Curious, I glanced back at the pond and visualized what needed to happen. Slowly, a blob of water rose as it glided across the surface. At the edge of the pond, it cut through tall blades of grass, and I lost control. It exploded into droplets and rained back down into the pond. I relaxed my shoulders, lifting my hand toward the water once more. This time it made it to the edge of the fire pit. By the third time, water had pooled in the grass. One last time I floated a blob toward the fire Grace had created. I held it for a moment, sensing my control of the element, before I dropped it and extinguished the flames. I beamed with pride and plucked my mother's sword from the chair.

"Ember!"

I turned at the sound of my name. Grace waved from

the door. We would spend the rest of the night watching episodes of *Gossip Girl*. I'd missed the last season, and it thrilled Grace to rewatch the show. I smiled as I hurried into the house to spend much-needed girl time, wishing Hannah could have been here with us.

We would find Hannah and bring her home.

Twenty-eight

EMBER

My head pounded against the constant beeping sound. *What the fuck is that?* I opened my eyes unwillingly, focusing in on the foreign yet familiar room. *Why does my head hurt so much?* I rubbed my eyes. An empty margarita bottle lay beside me. *Shit.*

The beeping continued. I dug through the blankets we laid out on her floor hours ago for our marathon. I snatched up the annoying phone. Grace's screen lit. I noticed two things. Four missed calls from Luke, and it was three in the morning.

"Grace!" I shrieked.

She rolled over beside me. "Quit yelling."

I stood, kicking at the wrapped bundle. "This is your fault."

"Stop *yelling,*" she hissed. "What's my fault?" she asked in a lower tone.

"We're late for the mission," I said as I looked for my

phone in the mess. That got Grace to move. She started to tidy the room. "We don't have time. We need to go. Now."

"Right," Grace said, slipping her hands into her shirt.

Grace grabbed my elbow as I was jumping into my pants. White light filled the room.

I closed my eyes against the bright light as nausea started clawing at my stomach. It took seconds to teleport into Parker Elementary cafeteria, but the quick sudden movements made me regret the drink Grace poured me.

It'll be fine. One margarita won't hurt you. I'll pour a small one.

When I opened my eyes, seven pairs of eyes stared back at me. I grimaced at the furious tick in Luke's jawline.

"Sorry," I muttered, but he ignored me.

Eyes drifted away from us, and I sighed in relief as I buttoned my pants. Grace moved farther into the room and sat down with Ted as she twisted her shirt around from back to front.

What've you been up to, love?

I locked eyes with Christo, who had a small smirk on his stupid face. *Wouldn't you like to know.*

It's why I asked? He sounded peeved, and I smiled.

Luke started talking, gaining everyone's attention. "Now that we're all *here,* we can get started. We don't have enough time to walk through the whole plan, so I'll just tell you I made changes."

I glanced at Luke. *Changes now?*

"Nathan will be going inside the house while Jasmine will stay outside with the others."

"You can't do that," Jasmine yelled.

She marched from the other side of the room to stand toe to toe with Luke. Her eyes locked with his.

"I can and will," Luke said, staring down at the Zodian woman. Jasmine only came to his shoulder. "Now, we only have a small window of time. We need to get moving."

Jasmine didn't back away as she lifted on her toes. "I need to be on the inside. I need to get my friend to safety."

Luke turned his attention back to Jasmine. "We don't have time to argue."

Sofia pulled Jasmine back as she huffed. Sofia nodded, and Luke started to count down. A hand slid into mine and squeezed.

Drink too much, love?

I eyed Christo, and my stomach did a different flip. Our eyes locked as the world seemed to fade around us. A stir started below, and I looked away, breaking the connection in time to hear the last of the countdown.

The fluorescent light shifted to darkness as we landed in tall grass. Sand slipped beneath my feet as my vision adjusted. The house before us sat dark, the moonless night making it hard to see in the distance. Chris pulled me to the ground. We hid in the tall grass, barely able to see the others. I kept my hand locked with Christo, the hold solid and comforting against the darkness surrounding us.

Rabon's not afraid of the dark, love.

But would there be others in the house? We were prepared for vampires and demons to be stationed outside. So the silence seemed weird.

"Everyone here?"

I sensed the aether around me, counting our team. The others sounded off over the crashing waves below. Something else was nagging in the back of my mind. *Why were there no other signatures around the area?* I knew the house was spelled, but could it block the aether?

"Luke," I whispered. "Something's off."

"This is our only chance," Sofia hissed.

Jasmine cut in, "We can't let this opportunity go to waste."

Luke drew closer to me. "What's wrong?"

How did I explain it to him? "Where are the guards?" I uttered.

"We'll figure it out," he said to me, then spoke louder to the group. "Everyone, keep your eyes peeled for anything out of the ordinary. Let's go."

The tingling of Christo's power surged up my arm as, once again, darkness shifted into bright light. We landed in the foyer of the house. Christo said there would be two staircases on either side that led to the balcony overlooking the ocean. What we didn't expect was the room full of vampires. *I was so right.*

Christo and Luke engaged the first few that came our way. Our two groups came together to take on the other vampires.

"Chris!"

Three vampires jumped onto his back. He spun around quickly, trying to knock them off, but they held on. He glanced my way.

Be right back.

He disappeared with the vampires.

"What's going on?" Nathan yelled. "How did they know we would be here?"

"I don't know," I answered as I watched more vampires dart in from the balcony. They were enclosing us into the corner.

Luke charged forward into the vampires, slashing and staking, but there were too many. They pinned him to the ground, and my heart leaped. Fire burst from my hands and expanded outward, swirling throughout the room. Nathan screamed as he grabbed hold of Kaity, pulling her away from me. Sofia made a wall of water, protecting herself.

"Shit." The fire exploded, leaving vampire dust in its wake. Flames trailed across the floor and up the curtains.

"You set my hair on fire!" Kaity screamed as she furiously patted down her head.

Luke's eyes widened as he climbed to his feet, coming toward me. "Are you okay?" he asked.

I opened my mouth to answer, but my words died when I spotted a man standing on the balcony. That familiar feeling washed over me again, but this time the aether delivered death and decay, defying that wholesome look. His blond hair shone in the darkness. He stood tall despite the fact he was leaning against the balcony railing. Torches lined the edge, casting shadows around him. He lifted his eyebrow in my direction, as if making a toast to me.

Ash settled on the ground as more vampires rushed in from other rooms.

"We need to get out of here," Luke said, wrapping his arm around me before glancing at where I stared.

His arm tightened as he made out the man on the balcony. The same man that had been at Parker Elementary school, who told Luke he was a *God,* and that he needed to act like one.

Sofia's voice cut through the chaos around me. "This is our only chance." She darted up the nearest stairs.

"Wait," I yelled before snaking out of Luke's hold and ascending after her.

Once we made it to the second level, more vampires waited.

"Em," a voice said beside me.

I glanced over at Nathan. He nodded, and we started down the corridor after Sofia.

"Where is she?" Sofia yelled ahead of us.

I conjured fireballs and threw them at the incoming vampires as Sofia pinned one to the wall. Her ice dagger pointed at his face.

"Where is she?" she shouted again.

I came to her side to protect her back. I held my arms up in preparation as more vampires sprinted from across the other side.

"Sofia, we can't take on this many," I pleaded with

her as Nathan and I blocked and dusted the ones that got close.

Sofia lessened her hold, and the vampire twisted, gained power, and threw her back. I grabbed her hand as she flew over the glass railing and managed to stall her descent. My lower body pressed into the glass, bending me at the waist as Sofia hung from my arm.

"Pull me up!" she yelled, swinging, gaining the attention of the vampires below her.

I turned to where Nathan had been, but he'd been pushed farther down the hallway by a couple of vampires. He locked eyes with me and nodded. I just needed to wait for him, and he would help.

"Ember, bring me up," Sofia shrieked from below.

"You're fucking heavy." I turned my attention back down to her as I inched my arm up.

I got her halfway where she could grab ahold of the railing to pull herself the rest of the way.

"Let me help," a voice said beside me.

Sofia and I froze as a hand reached down to grab her. She let go of the railing, sinking further down, dragging me with her. I slammed into the railing. She locked eyes with me. Fear shone through as I made a decision. I released her hand, letting her fall toward the bodies below.

The invading hand missed Sofia's by a split second as she fell to the first floor. I stood still as I watched her fall on top of several vampires, knocking them to the ground.

The arm rescinded. I straightened and turned to face the man from the playground.

"Well, that wasn't very nice." He smirked. "I wanted to play with her."

I shivered as I stepped back.

"Em," Nathan yelled from behind the monster before me.

He jumped, fist coming down.

The man turned and caught Nathan by the throat in one fell swoop. Nathan gripped the hand around his neck, twisting and pulling to break free.

I locked eyes with Nathan but heard the crunch of bones as I reached for him.

I gasped as Nathan's aether signature faded away. An instant. It took only an instant for Nathan to die.

"No!" I screamed, rooted to my spot.

Nathan hung limply in the man's hand. The man shrugged and tossed Nathan's body over the railing like a rag doll.

"Nathan," I yelled, but there was nothing I could do.

He was gone. It didn't seem real. He'd been giving me crap the last few weeks for ditching Luke, but I knew deep down it was just teasing. A lump formed in my throat, and my stomach twisted. Tears welled at the edge of my eyes, and heat brewed in my body.

I turned back to the monster before me.

His smile became lazy as he swept his blonde hair to one side, "Now, where were we? Oh yes, I guess I'll just have to play with you instead."

He lunged toward me. I sidestepped, bringing my hands up to defend. The force of his strike flung me farther back, my feet skidding against the marble as I tried to balance myself. He gave me no breathing room as he stalked forward. The force of his strikes sent shooting pain vibrating through my arms as I tried to block. I barely kept ahead of the hits, moving my feet to duck and dodge the blows.

"Hm, are you a Zodian knight then?"

"What?" I muttered, stumbling.

I tried to bring the flames forth, but only sparks appeared on my fingertips. *Shit.*

"A witch then." He aimed for my midsection.

I wasn't fast enough this time. The punch hit me full force. I coughed, doubling over as the contents of my stomach spewed out between us. He stepped back in disgust, looking at the speck on his shoe.

I wiped my mouth with my sleeve. The remnants of Bob's margarita mix burned my nostrils. I glanced at the monster, his face still distorted.

I wheezed, clutching my stomach. *This was my only chance.* I snapped my fingers, creating nothing but a spark. It fluttered.

He bent down to wipe the vomit off his Italian shoes. Once he rose, he flicked the handkerchief over the railing. "That wasn't very attractive. The moment you stepped inside my house, you signed the death warrants for your friends. I'll make you watch while I kill them all."

The heat grew inside me. I focused my energy on fueling each spark, igniting them into fireballs before I tossed them onto the floor. Whatever was in Bob's concoction still lingered in my vomit. It caught, and I continued to grow it into a bonfire pushing it in his direction. Once the fire turned bright blue, I sprinted down the hall behind me.

I headed around to the other side of the second floor, throwing fireballs at any incoming vampire, not giving them a chance to get close. When I ran past the glass window, I couldn't help but notice the stormy sea below. I could hear the waves crashing against the rock as lightning flashed in the distance.

I rounded the corner and looked down to see Sofia on her feet, fighting several vampires with Kaity and Luke nearby. The quickest way down was to go over the railing, but I stared down at the marble tile and thought better of it. I hurried toward the staircase, but I couldn't help looking over to see the fire still burning where I had left it, but no one was on that level anymore.

He's on my cheat list. I stopped and grasped the railing for support. *Hannah?* I surveyed the area. Hannah had to be close by if the aether was reminding me of this memory. I let my senses scan the aether around me.

The aether that circled back to me was confusing. I couldn't sense anyone on this floor with me, but that couldn't be. Hannah had to be close. I glanced back over the railing, locking eyes with Luke.

"We have to go," he shouted.

I shook my head. This was it. We would not get another chance to find Hannah. I wasn't leaving until I knew she was safe at home with Doug.

There were only two rooms on this side. I headed to the first door, turned the knob, and stood in darkness. I flicked my wrist, and a fireball appeared. I guided it to the middle of the room. A library or office. *Nothing.* But as I started to close the door, something caught the light of my fire. I made out a bookshelf against the back wall. The same bookshelf I had viewed through the portal in the cave. I was close. Hannah had to be here.

I stepped cautiously into the room. The fireball floated beside me as I moved around the outdated furniture. I shifted the fireball closer to the shelf. I squatted down, eye level with the spine of a book that reflected my flame. I pulled the leather-bound book slowly from the shelf, recognizing the same marks I'd seen on Sofia's and Jasmine's skin. I opened it and drew my fireball closer. The first page was blank. Nothing on the second page. I flipped through the book. Nothing but blank pages. I traced my finger over one of them, and ripples appeared, then writing.

"Wow."

The sounds of fighting filtered through the room, and I snapped the book shut. I slid it into the back of my pants and pulled my shirt down over it. I darted back through to the other room.

I pushed down on the door handle, but it was locked. *Could Hannah be in there?* I pulled a bobby pin out of my hair and knelt down. I'd successfully broken into my dad's room, but this lock was different. *We have a problem.* After several seconds of trying, I sensed decay drawing closer through the aether. I swiveled up to my feet, hands ready, fireball in each for whoever was there. But nothing. The fighting from below grew louder each minute. *I don't have time for this.*

I twisted back around and held my hand over the handle. A stream of fire appeared. The doorknob held strong for a split second, but the wood began to burn as the handle turned red hot. I kicked at the handle with all my might and watched it fall to pieces on the floor.

Terrified eyes greeted me from the other side. "Ember."

"Hannah." I tugged her into my arms. "I was so worried I would never see you again."

"Move," a voice yelled behind Hannah and then shoved her into me. I caught her before she fell to the ground. A young woman with black hair stood in the doorway. "Well, let's go," she said.

The fighting from below grew louder. "Yes, let's go. Down the stairs. My friends are waiting," I said, grabbing Hannah's hand to pull her along.

At the top of the stairs, I looked below to see bodies of demons and dust covering the marble tile. Luke, Kaity, and Sofia were grouped together in the same spot as earlier, holding their own against the onslaught of enemies.

"There." I pointed, and the three of us started down the stairs.

It took only seconds to descend, but the pounding of my heart accelerated. We were so close. Hannah was finally going to be safe.

We made it to the bottom; Luke and I made contact before he turned to punch a vampire. Sofia ran straight to the other Zodian with us. They hugged. My hand still linked with Hannah's, I pulled her along to Kaity's side.

"We need to get out of here," Kaity said, grabbing my arm. "Luke."

"Hannah, take Kaity's hand," I said, glancing behind me as more vampires filed out from other rooms. "Grab Kaity," I yelled to the others.

A small fire started beside me. The other girl we saved had her eyebrows scrunched and her lips tight as she held out her hand toward the fire, but it wasn't moving.

I flicked my wrist, adding my power to hers. The fire roared to life, encircling our small group and blocking the vampires from advancing.

"Let's go." I grabbed Hannah's hand, who had Kaity's.

Kaity's other hand connected with Sofia, who held on for dear life to the girl we rescued. Luke shifted beside me as he grasped mine.

Nathan's body lay at Kaity's feet. His eyes closed. He could have been sleeping it off if his neck wasn't at a weird angle. Would Kaity be able to take his body back to Ted? Kaity caught my eye and nodded. *Yes.* Light came from Kaity as her power surrounded us. I glanced around the room, the fire blocking my view.

Christo? Would he be all right?

I was yanked by my hair, shocked, and my body seemed to be suspended in the flames. Luke's eyes widened as my fingers slipped through his hands. A flash of light boomed throughout the room.

I flew back, shattering the glass door. It fell to the ground with me. Blood seeped down my neck. My hand trembled as I grazed the cut on the back of my head. My stomach lurched, my vision whirled, and my body ached. But before I could stand, a hand snaked through my hair, pulling me through the glass I lay in.

The cold voice whispered, "I wasn't done playing, Zodian."

Twenty-nine

LUKE

A sharp metallic scent seared my nostrils. Kaity disappeared with the others the exact moment Ember's hand had been jerked from mine.

I stood at the front of the house while he stood before the balcony doors, his fingers intertwined in Ember's hair. I growled, showing teeth for once. I scanned the area; the lackeys were back in the shadows giving their leader space.

He lifted Ember to her feet, and blood dripped from her scalp. My stomach tightened at the sight. He whispered something to her, and she tensed. He stared at me. The same cold eyes from that night at Parker Elementary.

He smirked. "You want a taste, brother?"

A growl grew in my chest. *Brother?*

That night at the playground, he had only spoken in cryptic messages, never revealing his identity, but here in this house, he had to be Rabon. I should have put the pieces together before now. At least I could have saved some of the women before it got this far.

"Again, we stand on two different sides," he said. "When will you learn that the winning side is my side?"

Ember whimpered. Her eyes glazed over in pain. She probably had a concussion from hitting the door. Glass shards littered the ground around her. I shifted my glance to Rabon, and his smile widened. He seemed to enjoy himself.

I widened my stance, scanning the room for a possible escape. I sensed his movement and turned back to him, smiling. His smile faltered for a second before it was replaced with a sneer.

I am going to break his fucking arm for hurting her.

I took a step forward. "We don't have to be on opposing sides."

"It looks that way to me, brother," he said, cocking his head.

That word again.

"We will remain on different sides as long as you help witches like her." He pulled Ember closer, sniffing her hair. "Though she does smell delicious." He licked the side of her neck where the blood dripped down from the gash on her head.

A growl rumbled in my chest again. I stepped forward, marking the halfway point between the foyer and the exit to the veranda.

Rabon laughed. "So you do want a taste. Why didn't you say so?"

He stepped back, dragging Ember with him. Her eyes were still not focused or alert.

I took two steps to his one as we exited the house onto the veranda. The waves crashed below, and a hint of blue lit the early morning sky.

"You could join me, brother."

I tensed as he switched hands, grasping Ember's neck with his other, letting her bloody hair fall over her face. She was so close to the ledge. *Would he kill her? Could I get to her before?*

"But you're not there yet. My plans are coming together quite nicely."

He lifted Ember, and her feet dangled beside him. The blood dripped from her shoes onto the pavement.

"I can help with your plans," I pleaded. "Just put her down."

Rabon lowered Ember as he looked at me, his eyes locked with mine, and he smiled. "Go fetch."

He flung Ember backward over the railing. She flew back and disappeared over the edge.

I pushed off with all my strength vaulting over the railing. I soared toward the waves crashing against the rocks below.

I reached for her as we free-fell.

"Ember," I whispered, desperate to reach her before she hit the rocks.

She opened her eyes, recognition in them as her hand reached toward mine. The lightning flashed around us as we fell. Her fingers touched mine. Fear filled me as we were both enveloped in a sphere of violet lightning. The air and static constricted. I pulled Ember closer to my chest as the ball of lightning shrunk around us, suffocating us in a bleach-like scent. Ember's eyes arced like lightning was glowing from her. The light erupted before darkness descended upon us.

Thirty

EMBER

Warmth spread through me as I awoke slowly. My head rose and fell with Luke's deep breaths. A familiar scent of ozone seared my nostrils. I opened my eyes to darkness but knew I was safe from *Rabon*. He had killed Nathan and kidnapped Hannah and hurt so many others. *He nearly killed me.*

I moved my arms and felt resistance as Luke's arms were wrapped around me. His breathing evened as he slept. I smiled at the thought of our favorite sleeping position all those years ago. He always made me feel wanted, just as myself.

His arms were hot against me, and one fell limp at his side. I looked down to see purple glowing from his forearm. I flicked my wrist, creating a fireball, growing it bigger to light up the space around us.

"Luke," I yelled, but he didn't stir, his breathing coming shallower and shallower. I turned onto my knees, taking his shirt in my hands. I shook him. "Luke!" His eyelids slowly crept open, and I sat back on my heels. "Oh my god." I sighed. "Are you okay?"

"Are you okay?" he asked, as his fingers brushed against the side of my head. "Your head stopped bleeding."

I grabbed his hand, turning it over. "What happened?"

Purple streaks glowed lightly from the skin on his forearm, resembling arcs of lightning.

He looked at the mark. "It must be from when the lightning hit you and passed through me." Luke's voice croaked. "Rabon hurt you. Dropped you off the veranda."

I touched his face. "You jumped off to save me?"

His face stilled under my fingers. "Of course, but that's when the lightning hit us. I don't understand." He looked around. "How did we end up at the school?"

The school? "I don't know. I thought you brought us here. But it's okay. It's over now."

His body tensed. "No, it's not over, Ember."

I didn't know what he meant. "But the women are safe."

Tension filled his body. "Rabon is still out there. He's planning something that has to do with the Zodian Warrior."

The Zodian Warrior. "We saved Jade. She's the warrior."

"How can you be sure?"

"Sofia and Jasmine told me the story. Jade's been groomed as the warrior her entire life."

"Hmm, you don't think they were the ones that leaked our plans?" he asked.

"They wanted to save their friend as much as we did. Why would they lie about a story?"

"Then there's Christo who gave us the information," Luke uttered.

"It wasn't him," I said without a thought.

"How do you know?"

"He was bound by his word to Sofia."

"Someone told Rabon we would be there."

"Who though?" I sat in contemplation for a moment.

Luke's fingers brushed my face, tenderly touching the parts that hurt. "I'm so glad you're okay," he whispered as if he hadn't believed it earlier.

I responded to the gentleness of his touch. "I'm sorry about Nathan." I knew that there had been nothing I could have done to save him, but I still felt responsible for his death.

Luke's hand gently lifted my chin to meet his eyes. "We will get through this. We'll honor Nathan by making Rabon pay."

I nodded, my face slipping out of his hold. "How do we take down someone who keeps coming back to life?"

"We first need to understand what he's after and why," Luke said. "Once we know that, we can find his weaknesses."

I opened my mouth to speak when a small red bubble popped up between us from the floor.

"What is that?"

I watched the ball as the light grew. "It looks like Kaity's Last Moments spell," I said.

"Whoa, what's going on here?" Christo said, appearing in the room. *Didn't you sense me?*

I looked at Chris and shook my head. He tilted his head as he looked down at us together.

Kaity came crashing through the doors a moment later. She stopped beside Christo. "Sheesh, we were gonna rescue you. I wanted to be the hero. But I guess someone already beat me to it."

"Why are you here?" Luke said, standing and, in turn, helping me.

"He appeared in the school after we got back and realized you two were missing. It seemed like a good idea in case you were captured by Rabon," Kaity answered.

Kaity made a good point. Luke sighed.

Luke asked, "Kaity, can you heal Ember's cut?"

Christo stepped closer to me, frowning as he checked my head. Kaity came over to me and placed her hands gently on my head. A dizzying sensation came over me as she used her magic to heal my wound.

Chris placed his hand on my lower back. *Check on you later, love.*

I nodded absently. Grief washed over me as he disappeared.

"We can't trust him," Luke said from my other side.

"Well, he did arrive here and offer to help find you two," Kaity countered.

"If he stayed at Rabon's to fight instead of leaving, we

might not have needed to be almost rescued," Luke huffed out.

I silently agreed as we trekked back into the cafeteria. I glanced around the empty room. "Where are Sofia and Jasmine? Grace? Hannah?"

Kaity's face fell. "Ted went home to figure out how to tell his aunt and uncle about Nathan. Grace's parents came home early, and she had to leave quickly. The other Zodians were overjoyed at finding their friend, Jade. They left almost immediately."

"Oh," I said.

Thankfully, I'd lived through the encounter with Rabon. Flashes of being thrown over the edge came back to me full force, and I pushed down my panic.

"Not a problem." Kaity hugged me before saying her goodbyes and vanished.

Bob must have gone home since the bar sat empty. I wished I had been able to speak to Hannah. Luke headed to the bar.

"Pour me one," I called to him as I pulled out the strange book I'd put in the back of my pants, surprised it was still there.

"I'm not bringing it over," Luke said after bottles clanked together.

I headed over, feeling more like myself after Kaity healed me. I took the drink from Luke. We tipped the drinks back, taking it in one shot.

I poured us another drink, attempting to erase the flashes from earlier.

"Rabon," I began turning toward Luke. "I heard him

mention his brother, Istros." I repeated the name Jasmine had used days ago.

He tensed beside me as his eyes widened.

"That's the second of the Chaos Brothers. If Rabon is this horrible, could his older brother be worse?"

Luke downed the shot. "I don't know."

His hand tightened around the glass, and it exploded into tiny pieces.

I grabbed his hand, checking it, but his skin was already healing itself. "It's going to be okay."

Luke nodded, and I took my shot. I sat the glass back on the counter.

It occurred to me that Grace had used her powers to bring us to the school earlier. Groaning, I asked Luke if I could borrow his truck again to drive out to Grace's place to retrieve my car.

The door creaked. *Awesome, maybe Grace remembered.*

Thirty-one

EMBER

I turned and met my dad's eyes. He stood in the entrance of the cafeteria, and even from this distance, I could see the vein in his neck bulging.

He walked farther in, and the room's low lights glistened off the faded pink box he carried.

The present neatly wrapped for my twenty-first birthday.

A chance to be normal.

A chance to have a life of happiness.

A chance to live, he said.

My salvation. The item Dad worked hard to find for me.

I tightened my fists at my sides; Luke stood silent beside me waiting for Dad to speak first.

He stopped a few feet from us. "Emma."

I cringed at the name, but he continued undisturbed. "What in the hell are you doing here? Mrs. Andrews stopped by the house earlier. I never dreamed she would hand me this. She said she found it in the back of Grace's closet. She didn't know how long it had been there but wanted to be sure you got it back. How in the hell did it get there in the first place?"

Flinching at the harshness of his words, I didn't answer right away.

"Emma." He thrust the pink box out at me. "You promised me you had taken this." Sadness crept into his eyes but vanished instantly. "This is your only hope."

I took the box from him. "It didn't feel right, Dad," I said, my voice loud and clear even as my hand shook. My pulse beat erratically under my skin.

"What? You don't know what right is. You're a monster."

Stunned, I didn't know what to say. My entire life, I'd been doing what Dad scheduled for me each and every day.

My voice came out stronger than I thought it would. "I couldn't get rid of those pieces of myself. You have no idea what it's like, feeling the powers that lie beneath, unable to grasp them. I barely functioned as a person. Going through each day based on what *you* wanted me to be, not what I truly am. The day my powers resurfaced was the day I felt alive again. I made the choice not to drink the elixir. I chose me. Helping the women in the cave escape their fate and finding Hannah solidified my choice. I've proven to myself that I am not a monster."

"You don't know what you are doing," Dad spat. "Open the box and take it right now."

I didn't budge to open the package.

I should have made this decision a long time ago. I gazed at my cure wrapped in pink and knew what I needed to do.

Dad reached for the box, but flames consumed it before he could touch the pretty white ribbon. Ashes fell to the floor. The liquid in the vial boiled, and the glass shattered into a million tiny pieces as I glanced at Dad.

"I choose to be a Zodian."

Dad stared at the shards on the floor. He whispered, "You don't know what you've done." And then he spoke louder, "I wanted you to be safe. I can't protect you anymore. You're bringing this on yourself." He stepped back, bumping into one of the tables, spinning around.

"What are you talking about?" Luke asked, standing beside me.

I'd nearly forgotten he was in the room. Dad looked back at Luke before turning to meet my eyes. "Zodians have been hunted to extinction by the Chaos Brothers and others for centuries. That will never change. Now that you have full access to your powers, it's only a matter of time before they track you down and kill you just like your mother. Your mother descended from the royal bloodline. You are the last of that line. I loved her, but I'm not going to let you break my heart like she did."

Confirmation. What Christo said was the truth. Everything I wanted Dad to tell me these past few weeks was out in the open. And now, those secrets were more curse than comfort.

Luke and I glanced at each other. *If Dad knew how close I'd been to Rabon tonight . . .*

"Dad." I didn't know where to begin. "Talk to me. We can work through this."

He shook his head, backing out of the room, his eyes wide with disappointment and anger. "I won't do this. Don't come home. I don't want or need you there." He met my eyes, turned, and walked out of my life.

"Dad," I yelled.

Don't come home.

This couldn't be happening. I knew he didn't like me having powers, but I loved him. Didn't he love me? He'd been my whole world. I didn't understand. How could he toss me out like old garbage? I was his child. Weren't all parents supposed to love their children unconditionally?

Warmth wrapped around me. "It'll be okay. You can crash here until he comes around," Luke said in my ear as he held me.

Tears slipped down my face, and I wiped them away. Would it be okay? I had my friends, but was that enough?

"Thank you," I whispered into Luke's shirt.

I had finally decided my fate, even though I'd known it all along.

Thirty-two

EMBER

I sat cross-legged on the concrete floor at the range, two days after Dad's outburst at Parker Elementary. He had yet to forgive me. My calls rolled to voicemail.

I hoped that he would come around in time, but I needed to continue on my journey. If what he said was true, the Chaos Brothers would try to kill me. I needed to be at my strongest. While I learned how my powers worked in general, fighting with them wasn't natural for me yet. I would need to train as hard and as fast as I could.

"What's up, kid?"

"I destroyed the elixir."

"Ah."

"Christo says I'm part of the royal bloodline, and Dad told me Rabon will kill me." I paused, letting that sink in. "I really need to start training hardcore if I'm going to survive."

Silence followed my statement. My gut tightened,

and heat spread through me. *Did she already know all of this?*

"You knew."

"No, not really, but I had my suspicions with your abilities."

"Why didn't you say anything sooner? You could have saved me a lot of trouble. Why is everyone always holding out?"

"Kid, I'm not trying to hide anything from you. I'm here for you always. You're my family."

"Do you know who the Zodian Warrior is?"

Lyra made a clicking sound, "That's a relatively new term."

"We saved the girl they thought was the warrior from Rabon." *Was she?* "But I don't think she is of the royal bloodline." I paused.

"I'm happy you burned the box. It's beyond time you stepped into yourself."

"Well, it wasn't pleasant. My dad," I started. *He called me a monster, breathe.* "Dad doesn't want me around anymore. He told me not to come home."

She sighed. "He'll change his mind, but in the meantime, I'll train you as much as I can."

"Thanks."

"No problem, kid. You know more than you think. It's getting your brain to turn off so you can access your powers that's going to be your biggest hurdle."

"How are we going to get past that?"

The aether constricted around me, and I glanced at

Christo standing at the edge of the concrete. One hand behind his back as he smiled down at me.

"I'll need to call you later."

Lyra mumbled bye, and I placed my phone on the table next to me, but as I stood to greet him, it vibrated. I glanced at the screen. *Grace, I'll call her back.* I pushed the ignore button before turning back to Christo.

"I know you're sad about your dad, but it'll work out." He brought his other hand from behind his back. He held a bow almost identical to the one I had lost in the cave. "I thought this would bring you a small happiness."

Warmth spread through me as I took the bow. Now in my hands, I could tell that it wasn't the exact same, but it was close. I pulled at the strings; they were strung tight, but with use, they would be workable.

"Thank you," I said. The immediate happiness slipped as confusion washed over me. It was a thoughtful gift, but it wouldn't bring Dad back to me.

The last few days had been busy, and I hadn't had time to process everything that happened. He hugged me. I sighed with pleasure at his mere touch. A moment later, he released me, and confusion then warmth hit me. This was what being with Christo was like, constantly fighting between the heat and ice. Christo's bond seemed to claw its way into my heart.

"I'll call you later," he muttered.

He left before I could respond. I tightened my hand around the bow, then looked down at my new gift. *Might as well put it to use.*

I gathered some arrows from the trunk of my car and

stood facing the targets. I pulled the bowstring back, but the tightness fought my strength, and I let it go. I took a deep breath and relaxed my shoulders. The second time the string pulled taut. The light above the target flickered as I released the arrow. I heard the echo of the thud before I fired two more at the same target.

I stretched my arms to work out the soreness before walking down the worn path I had made over the last few weeks. The light continued to flicker; I pulled the three arrows out as I reflected on the hits. When was the last time I missed the red zone?

The aether swirled around me. The lamp went dark. Emerald flashed in my mind, distracting me and delaying my swing to block the attack I sensed coming from behind. My feet slid back in the loose sand as the attacker grabbed the bow. I brought my other hand up with the arrows intent on stabbing. The attacker dodged the pointy ends and grabbed the shafts above my hand.

We struggled in the darkness. My attacker was dressed in black with his lower face covered, but I could see his piercing green eyes.

I pushed against his hold before pulling back on the bow and letting it go. It flung into his face, and I used the moment to jump back several feet. I threw a fireball. The attacker threw the bow and arrows away. He dodged my flames and flung his arm in my direction.

I produced another fireball, but a handful of dust flew in my face. I coughed, wiping at my eyes as the attacker advanced. I wheezed, tossing another fireball as he closed in. Avoiding it, he slid on the loose sand. Trying to right himself, he twisted left when he should have twisted right.

He landed on top of me as we tumbled through the sand. The air was knocked out of me. The light flickered on above us. The attacker's face covering had been displaced. I stared up at the beautiful green eyes.

"Ember?" Those eyes filled with shock.

"Kitley?" I coughed again.

He looked down at me, his eyes widening, and warmth pooled low as I stared into his eyes. He rolled off, climbing to his feet. I sat up. He stood only a few feet away.

"Kit, what the hell are you doing?" I asked, but he closed his eyes and darted away.

I reached over in the grass to pull the new bow Christo had given me. It dangled, broken in two. *Stupid Jerk.*

To be continued...

The Lost Chapter
EMBER

I glared up at the blazing California sun. *December wasn't usually this hot.* I shifted, swiping the sweat from my forehead. *Gross.* I wiped it on my pant leg, turning to look at Vanessa. She'd been a solid friend the past two years, helping me cope with university life and losing Luke. Today, she was bundled in a thick turtleneck, a long button-down coat, and thick blue jeans. *How was she not hot?*

"Ember." Vanessa tugged on my arm, turning me toward our dorm. "I think Mrs. H is looking for us."

I glanced down the sidewalk to see the admin on duty standing outside the dorm with someone. She waved at us and then pointed in our direction.

"Go see what she wants so we can start celebrating your birthday." Vanessa switched her weight from one foot to the other and then back.

I headed down the path to meet Mrs. H. The young

man towered over the admin, easily clearing six feet. He wore black clothes, which amplified the golden gleam of his russet complexion. As I got closer, I could make out a name tag and a red cross-shaped emblem on his bicep.

"Ember, glad I caught you before you left," said Mrs. H. "This man has a delivery for you." She turned to the young man. "Now that we've found her, I'm getting out of this chilly air." She turned back toward me. "Make sure you ladies are home before curfew."

"Don't worry, Mrs. H, we plan to stay in town with Vanessa's cousin tonight."

She patted my shoulder. "Be safe then." And she headed back toward the dorm.

I turned to the man beside me, who'd stood silent during our exchange.

I took a closer look at the emblem on his sleeve. Blood red. It wasn't typical. It consisted of four crosses that connected at the center.

His green eyes pierced me. My breath caught, and my cheeks warmed even further. He smiled down at me as I averted my gaze to read his name tag.

"Kitley," I muttered aloud, coming back to his face.

His smile grew, and my knees wavered under me.

"Kit," he replied. "I have a package for you." He unzipped his top coat.

"Woah, buddy." I pushed my hands to catch the zipper. He stilled the moment our hands touched. I peeked up at his face. "What are you doing?"

Kit tried to open his jacket again. "I have something for you."

"I bet you do," I said.

Continue reading *The Lost Chapter* by signing up for my newsletter.

Bob's Margarita
Attempt #13

Components

1.5 oz Tequila

1 oz Fresh Squeezed Lime Juice

.5 oz honey simple syrup or agave nectar

Mix together, salt rim of glass with coarse salt, pour and garnish with lime.

Bob's topper - pineapple juice

Drink Responsibly

About the Author

First, I just want to thank you for reading Ember's story. It means the world to me. Don't worry, I'm working on the next one in between family time with my husband, two sons, and various four-legged creatures.

I started writing because I was dissatisfied with an ending to a story once, and that was that. I picked up my ball-point pen and started writing on legal pads. Eventually, I moved to typing, and once the words flowed, magic was created.

Join my community and follow me

Acknowledgments

I first want to thank myself for stepping outside my comfort zone and signing up for Publish and Thrive course by Sarra Cannon. Through this course, I learned so much and gained friendships I didn't know I was missing until now. I met my critique partners within this group, and I know that this book wouldn't have been possible without them. They have encouraged and taught me so much in the last two years. Alyssa Green has sparked my creativity when I thought none was there, Brittany M Riley is a pro at understanding commas and tech, while Lana Staux asks those hard questions to get the best story out of me. They are wonderful, and I just want to thank them from my heart for their friendship.

I want to thank my husband for taking on more responsibility during my writing times and always believing that I could do this when I didn't.

Also want to thank the authortube community for getting me excited about writing again.

See you in the next one . . .